On Your Mark, Get Set ...

I turned and tested out the new leather seat of my bike.

"Just do me one favor, Frank," Dad said when I reached for the ignition. "Don't take this new mission too lightly. They must have named it 'Extreme Danger' for a reason."

"That's what I told Joe."

"Well, be careful," said Dad.

Joe and I slipped our helmets over our heads and revved up our engines. Then, waving good-bye to Dad, we roared out of the parking lot and headed down the highway.

THE HARDY BOYS

UNDERCOVER BROTHERS™

#1 Extreme Danger

Available from Simon & Schuster

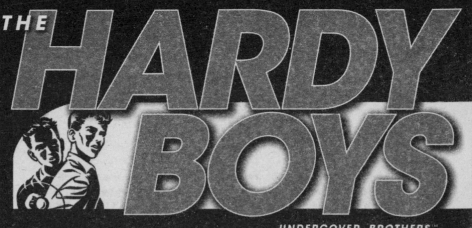

THE HARDY BOYS

BOYS

UNDERCOVER BROTHERS™

#1   **Extreme Danger**

FRANKLIN W. DIXON

Aladdin Paperbacks
New York   London   Toronto   Sydney

ALADDIN PAPERBACKS
An imprint of Simon & Schuster
Children's Publishing Division
1230 Avenue of the Americas
New York, NY 10020

Copyright © 2005 by Simon & Schuster, Inc.

THE HARDY BOYS MYSTERY STORIES is a trademark of
Simon & Schuster, Inc.
ALADDIN PAPERBACKS, HARDY BOYS UNDERCOVER BROTHERS, and colophon are registered trademarks of Simon & Schuster, Inc.

Designed by Lisa Vega
The text of this book was set in Aldine 401BT.
Manufactured in the United States of America
First Aladdin Paperbacks edition June 2005
10 9 8 7 6 5 4 3 2 1
Library of Congress Control Number: 2004113061
ISBN 1-4169-0002-0

TABLE OF CONTENTS

Extreme Danger

1.

Terror at 12,000 Feet

I'm going to die.

That's what I thought when I pulled the cord of my parachute—and nothing happened.

Definitely not cool.

As I plummeted downward through the sky, it felt like I was floating. The earth below, on the other hand, was rushing up to greet me at a speed of 120 miles per hour.

To make matters worse, it was my first solo jump.

And probably my last.

I tried not to panic. I looked over at "Wings" Maletta, the jumpmaster of Freedombird Skydiving School. The big bearded man was Freedom-falling about ten yards away from me. I waved to him like a maniac, pointing at my broken parachute cord.

And guess what he did?

He *laughed.*

Seriously. Like some sort of cartoon villain on Saturday morning TV, he threw his oversized head back and *laughed.*

Then it hit me.

He knows who I am.

In case you haven't figured it out, I'm no ordinary thrill-seeker who jumps out of planes. I'm Joe Hardy—undercover agent for ATAC (American Teens Against Crime)—and I was on a mission. A pretty dangerous mission, as it turned out. The police had reason to believe that the Freedombird Skydiving School was just a front for a fly-by-night smuggling ring. Wings Maletta wasn't a real diving instructor—he was a DVD pirate. So the ATAC team asked my brother Frank and me to go undercover to crack the case.

Hey, why not? Who would suspect a couple of teenage boys taking skydiving lessons?

Wings Maletta, that's who.

I stared at the broken pull cord in my hand and the big-toothed grin on Wings's round furry face. He looked right at me—then pointed up at the plane.

My brother Frank stood in the open doorway, getting ready to jump.

"Frank! Wait! Don't jump!" I shouted through the walkie-talkie in my helmet.

Too late.

Frank leaped out of the plane.

"They're onto us, Frank!" I yelled. "Maletta cut the pull cords!"

I waited for a response.

Nothing.

"Frank! Can you read me?"

Static.

I didn't know what to think. Did Frank hear me? Did someone sabotage his parachute too?

One thing I *did* know. If I didn't grab onto Wings Maletta in the next few seconds, I was going to be digging *really* deep for clams in the sandy beach below.

And I *hated* clams.

So I angled my body headfirst toward the dude who wanted to kill me—and tried to "swim" after him.

Hey, it works in the movies.

But this wasn't a movie. This was real life, and I didn't have a stunt double.

I didn't even get five feet before a wicked blast of air sent me spinning off course. I quickly straightened my arms into a diving position and managed to catch a "wave" of wind. Before I knew it, I was sailing right toward my target.

It was almost like body surfing, except I was swallowing mouthfuls of air instead of water.

And, oh yeah, my life depended on it.

Like a human rocket, I zeroed in on Wings Maletta and—*pow*—the guy didn't even know what hit him. I plowed into his bulging beer belly with a soft thud. Then, throwing my arms around his barrel chest, I held on tight.

Wings was totally stunned. You should have seen his face. With his eyes bulging in his goggles and his furry beard poking out of his helmet, he looked like a very large—and very confused—teddy bear.

Except teddy bears don't usually throw punches when kids hug them.

Whack!

Wings's huge hairy fist slammed into my jaw and sent me flying backward.

Man! That hurt!

It was still daylight, but I was seeing stars. And clouds. And the earth, too—spinning around me.

Time to get a grip.

I spread out my arms and legs to steady myself, then tilted downward. Wings reached for his parachute cord.

Oh, great.

If I didn't grab onto him in the next second or

two, I was going to plunge to my death. Not an option.

So I bucked against the wind like a wild bronco and thrust myself headfirst at Wings. With all my strength I lunged at him with my right arm.

Somehow I managed to grab his wrist—before he could pull the cord.

All right!

But Wings wasn't having it. He tried to brush me off like a bug, smacking my hand and swatting me away. I reeled back from his blows.

Then my hand started to slip off his wrist. One inch. And another.

Get a grip, I told myself again. But this time I meant it. Literally.

Suddenly the walkie-talkie in my helmet crackled with sound.

"Joe! Hold tight!"

It was Frank!

I glanced up. There he was! Swooping down like a bomber plane!

I grabbed onto Wings Maletta with both hands—and braced myself.

Wham!

Bull's-eye.

Frank crashed into us with shocking force. The collision sent the three of us tumbling through the air like a clumsy circus act. Frank clung on piggyback-style while I swung from my arms. And Wings? He kicked and screamed with every twist and turn.

"Get off me, you brats!" he howled. "The chute won't hold us all!"

I pulled myself up until we stopped spinning. But Wings wouldn't stop yelling.

"You idiots!" he bellowed. "When I pull the cord, you'll be flung off! You don't stand a chance!"

"Oh, no?" Frank shouted back. He held up a pair of tandem cords and clipped both of us to Wings's backpack.

I had to hand it to Frank. That kid is always prepared.

Wings let out a sigh. "We're still too heavy," he shouted.

"Just pull the cord," I said.

Wings shrugged—and pulled.

Whoomp!

With a massive jolt, Frank and I were ripped away from our bear-sized enemy. We plummeted downward, then shot back up again, held by the tandem cords. The parachute opened above our heads, but it sagged with our weight. In seconds we were drifting toward the drop zone below.

Problem was, we were drifting too fast.

"I told you," Wings grunted. "At this speed, we'll all die!"

Frank and I ignored him as we scrambled up the cords and grabbed onto Wings's legs.

"Let go!" the phony instructor yelled, trying to kick us off. "One of you has to let go—if you want to save your brother!" he added.

I looked Frank in the eye. I knew what he was thinking: *No way. We're a team.*

"I have another idea, Wings," I said, shimmying my way up the guy's body. "Maybe you can break our fall."

Wings cursed. I ignored him and straddled his thick neck. Then I reached down to help my brother until we were both standing on Wing's shoulders, holding the parachute lines for support.

"But wait! The fall could kill me!" Wings protested as we floated swiftly to the field below. "I'll break my legs, for sure!"

I glanced at my brother and shrugged. "That's a risk we're willing to take," Frank said with a smile.

The earth was only a couple hundred feet below us. Wings was freaking out. "No! My legs! I'll be crushed!"

"I have a suggestion, Wings," I said.

"What's that?"

"Tuck and roll."

As it turned out, Wings *did* break his legs in the fall. Which made it impossible for him to run away when the police arrived. They'd been watching the whole thing from the ground—and had an ambulance waiting to pick up the pieces.

I was just happy that none of the pieces had "Hardy" written on them.

"Good job, boys," said Lieutenant Jones, smiling and shaking our hands. "Sorry we got here a little late. By the time we realized your cover was blown, you were already in the air with Maletta."

"I can't believe that guy actually tried to kill us," Frank said, shaking his head.

"Well, he *is* a pirate," I pointed out.

"A *DVD* pirate," Frank added. "It's like he made us walk the plank for a bootleg copy of *Spider-man 6*."

I laughed. "Hey, we survived," I said, punching his arm.

Frank returned the favor by pushing me off-balance.

"You boys need a lift back to the skydiving school?" Lieutenant Jones asked, opening the door of his squad car.

"No, thanks. We're undercover," Frank explained. "Some kids from our school showed up for diving lessons today."

The police officer nodded and said good-bye.

Five minutes later Frank and I reached the Freedombird Skydiving School. We were totally beat, not to mention a little bruised. But it felt good to complete another successful mission. Wings and his smuggling ring were safely behind bars. And the Hardy brothers were ready to relax and chill out with some friends.

Unfortunately, Brian Conrad was the last "friend" we wanted to see—and the first person to spot us approaching the Freedombird School.

"Why did Brian have to show up for lessons today?" I moaned to my brother. "Talk about a bad coincidence."

"More like Murphy's Law," Frank chipped in.

"Hey, Hardys!" our least favorite classmate yelled from the parking lot. "I saw you jump. What's up with the double tandem diving? You girls get scared, or what?"

I glanced at Frank and rolled my eyes.

Let me tell you about Brian Conrad. The guy is like that public access TV—nothing but bad news, twenty-four seven. If the yearbook committee was voting for Boy Most Likely to Need a Good Lawyer, he'd win, hands down.

Of course, he hated Frank and me. In case you hadn't noticed.

"Too scared to go solo, huh?" Brian taunted as we approached the school building.

I growled under my breath.

"Ignore him, Joe," my brother whispered. Then Frank looked Brian in the eye and said, "Our parachutes malfunctioned, Conrad. We almost died."

"Yeah? I almost believe you," Brian shot back. He leaned against his SUV and shouted to his sister in the backseat. "You hear that, Belinda? Your boyfriends are too scared to jump solo! What a pair of wimps!"

Belinda glared at her brother. She opened her mouth to say something—but she was interrupted by a high-pitched voice inside the school building.

"Wimps! Wimps! Wimps!"

Brian Conrad burst out laughing.

Frank and I turned toward the small brick building and exchanged puzzled glances. We didn't know who it could be. The police had rounded up all of Wings's men. So we headed for the door and carefully peeked inside.

"Wimps!"

The sound came from a large gold cage in the corner.

It was Wings's pet parrot—the official mascot of the Freedombird Skydiving School.

"Figures," I muttered. "The pirate had a parrot."

Frank entered the small reception room and walked to the cage. "Poor thing," he cooed to the red and green bird. "Your daddy's behind bars now. Just like you."

The parrot tilted its head as if it understood.

"Maybe we should set you free." Frank opened the cage door and the bird flew out.

I ducked as it fluttered past my head. "Easy there, flyboy," I said.

The parrot circled the room a few times—and landed on Frank's head.

"Looks like you have a new friend, Frank," I said.

Frank rolled his eyes upward. The bird squawked.

And then Brian Conrad walked in.

"What do we have here?" the jerk sneered. "One parrot and a pair of chickens!" He pointed and laughed.

Okay, stay cool, I told myself.

If my brother and I could survive a parachute

jump without pull cords, we could put up with Conrad's obnoxious jokes.

But come on. Did the bird have to join in, too?

"Chickens! Chickens! Chickens!"

2.

Duck!

"I can't believe you really want to keep that bird," my brother Joe complained as we headed for the parking lot. "It keeps making fun of us."

I held the bird with one arm and opened the car door. "It's a parrot, Joe," I said. "That's what parrots do. They repeat things. And the poor thing is an orphan now. It needs a home." I gently placed the bird on the backseat of our Aunt Trudy's old Volkswagen Beetle.

Joe slid into the passenger seat and sighed. "But why couldn't it say 'Heroes! Heroes!' instead of 'Wimps! Wimps!'?" he asked.

The parrot flapped its wings. "Wimps! Wimps! Wimps!" it squawked.

I laughed while Joe closed his eyes and

groaned. "It's just so annoying," he said.

"It's only a bird, Joe," I reminded him again.

"I'm not talking about the parrot," Joe explained. "I mean, dude, we jump out of a plane with busted parachutes, take on a killer at twelve thousand feet, smash an international smuggling ring . . . and then get teased by a windbag like Brian Conrad."

"Hey, that's the price we pay for going undercover, Joe," I said. "And don't worry about Conrad. We won't have to see his face again till school starts in the fall."

Aunt Trudy's car engine died as soon as I tried to start it. And guess who we had to get a ride home from?

Brian Conrad.

I guess I spoke too soon.

I had to wave the guy down before he pulled out of the parking lot. Needless to say, my brother was not thrilled.

"Okay, I'll accept a ride home from that kid," Joe muttered under his breath. "But you owe me. Big time."

Brian's SUV screeched to a stop next to Aunt Trudy's dusty VW. "You boys need to be rescued twice in one day, huh?" he teased us yet again.

"Why are you driving that toy car, anyway?"

"Our motorcycles are getting a tune-up, Conrad," Joe said defensively.

I told my brother to chill out while we loaded our stuff into Brian's SUV.

"At least you get to sit in the backseat with your girlfriend," Joe whispered to me.

"Don't even start," I warned, my face turning red.

I guess I should explain. Brian's sister, Belinda, is smart, funny, blond, beautiful—the whole package. And she smiles and touches my arm every chance she gets.

Problem is, I get a little flustered around girls.

"Jump in, Frank," Belinda said, opening the rear door of the SUV. She flashed a smile that made me feel weak in the knees.

Okay, maybe I get more than just a little flustered.

Joe hopped into the front seat next to Brian. I knew the little creep grabbed shotgun just so he could watch me squirm next to Belinda.

I tried to play it cool as I slid into the backseat—with a parrot on my shoulder.

Real cool.

We fastened our seatbelts and Brian peeled out of the parking lot like it was the Indy 500. "Um,

15

we're not really in such a hurry, Brian," I pointed out.

"Sorry, I forgot the Hardys are allergic to danger," he said, slowing down only slightly.

"Put a lid on it, Brian," Belinda scolded her brother. "They were almost killed today. I hope you're all right, Frank." She placed a hand on my forearm.

"Well, yeah . . . um . . . it was . . . you know . . . a little scary," I stuttered.

What a dork.

"Don't worry. I'm fine," I said, clearing my throat.

Brian started clucking like a chicken, which caught the attention of the parrot on my shoulder. It raised its feathered head and squawked.

"I like your bird," Belinda commented with a smile.

I blushed. "Oh, yeah. Wings had to go to the hospital, so we're taking care of his pet."

"What's his name?" she asked.

I shrugged. "I'm not sure."

"Didn't Wings call him Birdbrain?" Brian said with a nasty laugh.

The parrot ruffled his feathers and made a loud raspberry sound.

"I wouldn't like that name either," I said to my

new feathered friend. The bird responded by poking my head with its beak.

Belinda giggled. "How about calling him Pokey?" she suggested.

The parrot puffed up its chest.

"Puffy?" Joe chimed in.

"Polly?" Brian added.

The bird squawked back. "Pokey! Puffy! Polly!"

"Man, he's like a tape recorder with wings, isn't he?" I said. "I guess I can throw away my digital mixing board. With this bird on my shoulder, who needs playback?"

The parrot flapped its wings with excitement. "Playback! Playback! Playback!" it chirped.

"That's it!" said Belinda, slapping my knee. "You can call him Playback!"

"Totally," Joe agreed.

"Okay. Playback it is," I said, petting the parrot's belly. I turned to Belinda and made a lame attempt at flirting. "I think he likes the name. I mean, who wouldn't . . . you know . . . like your . . . um . . . bird name."

Real smooth.

"It's perfect," I added, trying not to blush. I gave Belinda a cool sideways glance and nodded shrewdly.

Saved!

Well, until the parrot decided to poop on my shoulder.

"Gross," I muttered.

Everyone burst out laughing.

But really, did they *have* to make jokes about it the entire ride home?

"It's a parrot, Frank. That's what parrots do," my brother said, mocking my own words.

Belinda offered her sympathy—and a pack of tissues from her purse—but, boy, was I relieved when Brian pulled up in front of our house.

"Thanks, Brian," said Joe, hopping out and dashing to the porch of our old house. It was clear to everyone that Joe really hated thanking Brian for *anything*. He just wanted to make a quick escape.

Which left me alone with Belinda in the back-seat.

"You take care of yourself, Frank," she said. "You had a rough day, poor guy."

Then she gave me a peck on the cheek.

I'm sure my face turned redder than Playback's tail feathers. "Um . . . well . . . thanks, Belinda," I stammered. "And, ah, thanks for the ride, Brian."

Before I could embarrass myself any further, I ran up the porch stairs as fast as I could. I followed Joe into the house—and almost crashed right into him.

The entire family was sitting in the dining room, staring at us. Mom, Dad, Aunt Trudy—and they all had strange, surprised looks on their faces.

"Is that a parrot?" Mom asked.

"Parrot! Parrot! Parrot!" Playback responded.

Mom chuckled. "I guess that answers my question," she said. "I suppose you boys want to keep him?"

"Can we, Mom?" I replied. "He needs a home."

Aunt Trudy was horrified. "Is he housebroken?"

"Of course he is," I lied.

I might have gotten away with it if Playback hadn't chosen that exact moment to drop a little gift on my shoulder.

"I knew it!" Aunt Trudy exclaimed. "He's going to poop all over our nice clean house! When I was a little girl on the farm, we had some ducks and that's all they ever did. Poop, poop, poop all over the place."

"He's not a duck, Aunt Trudy," I argued. "And I promise to clean up after him."

Aunt Trudy stood up and started clearing plates off the table. "I think we all know who does the cleaning up around here," she said. "Not to mention cooking for a pair of boys who are always late for dinner."

"Sorry, Aunt Trudy," Joe and I said in unison.

Mom stood up, came over to me, and petted the parrot. "Isn't he a pretty thing?" she said. "I guess you can keep him, but he's your responsibility. I'll download some parrot info from the Web tonight for you."

"Thanks, Mom," I said, kissing her cheek.

I glanced at Dad. I could tell he was concerned about the skydiving mission. But we'd have to talk about it later, when Mom and Aunt Trudy weren't around.

"Did you pick up some Band-Aids for me?" Aunt Trudy questioned us.

Oops.

That was the reason Aunt Trudy had lent us her VW. "Um, there's something I have to tell you about your car, Aunt Trudy," I said, wincing. "The engine died on us."

"Yup," Joe confirmed.

"Well!" she said, shaking her head. "You know, something's fishy here. I send you boys out with my Beetle to buy some Band-Aids, and you come back with bruises and a bird. What *really* happened?"

Joe and I glanced down at the bruises on our legs.

"We'll tell you all about it . . . after you warm up some leftovers for us, Aunt Trudy," said my brother, thinking fast. "Thanks! We need to wash up first."

We both gave our aunt a kiss and bounded up the stairs before she could ask any more questions. Playback clung to my shoulder and squawked.

When we reached the second floor, Joe turned to me and said, "Well, Frank, I bailed you out of that one. You owe me again."

I swatted the back of his head and followed him into my bedroom. "Where are we going to put this bird until we get a cage?" I asked.

Joe walked to the window and turned around. "Let's see. We could push a couple of chairs together, and—"

I stopped listening, because something outside the window caught my eye.

A big red brick sailed through the air. Right toward our window.

"Joe!" I yelled. "DUCK!"

3.

Extreme Danger

Duck?

I ducked.

A split second later, something sailed past my head and crashed on the bedroom floor. I looked up to see what it was.

A brick?

I slowly raised myself to the window and peeked outside. The yard below was empty. Whoever threw the brick was gone.

"It's clear," I told Frank.

"Hey, want to give me a little credit here?" asked Frank. "It's a good thing I told you to duck—or you'd have another rock in your head."

"Very funny. But if you're so smart, why didn't you pick another word besides *duck*? I mean, dude,

22

after all the jokes today about ducks and chickens and parrots, I didn't know what you were talking about."

"What should I have said?" Frank asked. "Stoop? Bend? Lower yourself into a safe position? Hey, you figured it out. Now you owe me one."

"Let's just say we're even," I said. "Now stoop or bend down and check out that brick."

Frank leaned over and picked it up. The brick was your basic red brick—nothing unusual. But it was tied to a small padded envelope.

"What's that?" I asked. "A death threat from Brian Conrad? 'Stay away from my sister or the bird gets it. . . .'?"

Frank stood up. "No, it's our next mission."

He opened the envelope and pulled out a wad of cash, a hotel reservation, a small laser pointer, and a CD.

"Very clever," said Frank, turning the CD around in his hand.

"What's it say on the label?" I asked.

Frank looked me in the eye. "'Extreme Danger,'" he said.

"Cool," I replied, nodding. "But not as cool as this." I snatched the laser pointer out of Frank's hands and snapped off the lights.

Then, aiming toward the wall, I pressed the end

of the pointer with my thumb. A tiny pinpoint of light danced across the room.

Playback squawked.

With a flutter of wings, the large bird flew off Frank's shoulder and chased the pinpoint from one side of the room to the other. It was pretty hilarious watching Playback go. By swirling the laser, I could even make him fly in a perfect circle above our heads!

"Okay, knock it off," said Frank.

"But he likes it," I insisted.

"Joe."

"Okay." *Fun* wasn't in my brother's vocabulary. I aimed the laser above the TV set until Playback came to rest on top of it.

The parrot touched the tip of his beak to the pinpoint of light and screeched so loud it made me jump.

"Look!" said Frank. "The laser is burning a hole in the wall! Quick, turn it off!"

I released my thumb. The pinpoint of light disappeared instantly, but it left a small burn mark on the wall.

"Give me that," said Frank, snatching the pointer away from me and snapping on the lights. "Make yourself useful, Joe. Turn on the game player."

"Hey, I'm useful," I said, reaching for the game

controls. "I figured out we can use the laser pointer to burn holes, didn't I?"

"Yeah, and you almost burned a hole in my bird."

I had to bite my lip to keep from laughing.

"All set," I said, taking the CD from Frank and loading the game player. We plopped down on the beanbag chairs in front of the monitor and prepared ourselves for our next mission.

Bring it on.

I pressed PLAY.

The picture turned black. A low electronic hum grew louder and louder until it sounded like a chorus of spinning wheels. Suddenly the wheel sounds screeched to a halt, and two red slash marks crisscrossed the screen to form a giant X. Then there was a sizzling noise—like the sound of a burning fuse—and a huge explosion. The giant X burst into a fireball of tiny cartoon flames.

"Killer graphics," I said.

"Shhh," Frank responded.

The flames burned a bunch of holes in the screen, revealing a dozen little scenes—videostream clips of people skateboarding, bungee jumping, rock climbing, motocross racing, you name it.

"Extreme sports," a deep voice boomed over the soundtrack. "Pushing the limits of human skill and endurance, extreme sports have taken America by storm. Daredevil skateboard stunts, motocross mega-races, Big Air ramp-jumps, death-defying bungee dives—these are just a few of the pumped-up thrills that have captured an entire nation of brave young risk-takers. The highs are higher, the lows are lower, and the dangers . . . are extreme."

"Man, look at that ramp!" I said, slapping Frank's knee. "That must be fifty feet high! How can anyone—" On the screen a leather-jacketed motocrosser flipped backward on his bike and crashed headfirst on the ground.

"Oh, man! Wipeout!"

"Ouch," said Frank.

"Extreme events are more popular than ever," the deep-voiced narrator continued. "Once an underground phenomenon, extreme sports now receive international television coverage. Extreme Olympic-style games and events are popping up all over the world."

"Cool. Let's go," I said.

"Careful what you wish for," Frank warned. "You might end up flying over that fifty-foot ramp."

"Piece of cake."

I turned my attention back to the screen. The

videostreamed sports footage was suddenly replaced with tourist shots of Philadelphia.

"Philadelphia, Pennsylvania. Birthplace of the American Constitution," the voice went on. "City of Brotherly Love, home of the Liberty Bell. And proud host of the Big Air Games, the newest and biggest extreme sports competition in the country. If you are interested in this exciting midsummer event, tickets are still available. Hotel rooms are conveniently located, with all-day shuttle service to and from the stadium. Just call our 800 number located at the bottom of the screen. Be sure to ask about our special group rates."

I looked at Frank. "What is this? A commercial?"

"Sure sounds like it," he agreed. "All it needs is a catchy jingle."

Then another voice came from the speakers. It sounded like it was making fun of the narrator. "If you would like to attend the Big Air Games as an undercover agent, however, please press CONTINUE and you will be briefed on your mission."

"*That's* more like it," I said, grabbing the controls and pressing the button.

"Somebody at the home office must have a sense of humor," said Frank.

The tourist shots disappeared. A detailed map of Philadelphia filled the screen.

"Hello, boys," said the second voice. "Sorry about that introduction. I just thought I'd show you the tourist board's ad for the Big Air Games. We got you both tickets for all the events and reserved a room at the Four Seasons Hotel in Philadelphia."

A yellow square flashed on the map, indicating the hotel's location.

"Some of the top extreme athletes in the country are coming to the games—and staying at your hotel. Because of the size of the event, we're taking extra precautions. In dangerous times like these, it's important to always be prepared for the possibility of trouble. As teenagers, you'll be able to access more information than police officers could. Blend in, mingle with the fans and the athletes. But always, keep your eyes and ears open."

This was going to be great!

Frank didn't seem as excited. "It doesn't sound like much of a mission," he muttered. "Just hang out and watch other people take risks?"

"One more thing, boys," the voice spoke up. "We have reason to believe that several threats have been made to participants. Some skateboarders claim they saw a few strange postings on one of the extreme sports Web sites. There are thousands of those sites. The feds are checking the threats out, but it could take months to find something. Ask around. Gather all the information you can. I suggest you pack and leave as soon as possible."

I glanced at Frank. He sighed.

"This mission, like every mission, is top secret," the voice went on. "In five seconds this CD will be reformatted into an ordinary music CD. Five, four, three, two, one."

The Beastie Boys blared from the speakers.

The music was so loud it scared Playback off the TV. He flapped his wings and flew into the air, then landed on Frank's shoulder. He looked a little shaken. But after a moment or two he was grooving to the beat—and squawking the lyrics.

"Party! Party! Party!"

Frank walked over to the computer, turned it on, and logged in.

"What are you doing?" I asked. "We're supposed to leave as soon as possible."

"I'm going online to search some of those Web sites," he replied. "I'll only be a few minutes."

"Are you kidding?" I said. "The feds are looking for those threats day and night, and you think you can find them in a few minutes?"

"Hey, I'm the Search Master, remember?" he said, tapping his head with a finger. "My Web search talents are unmatched . . . except maybe by

Mom. But she's a librarian. It's part of her job."

"Sometimes I wish we could ask her to help," I said.

"Don't even think it. We're undercover, remember? We're on our own," he said, hunkering over the computer.

While Frank launched his Web search, I went to ask Dad to drive us to the garage to pick up our motorcycles. He was sitting by himself at the dining room table.

"Another mission? Already?" he whispered, looking up from his newspaper. "You haven't even told me about the last one."

"We'll fill you in later, on the way to the garage. Don't worry, Dad," I said, noticing the concerned look on his face. Then I turned around and headed back upstairs.

Frank hadn't moved since I'd left him.

"Find anything, O Mighty Search Master?" I asked.

Frank squinted at the screen. "I don't know. Maybe. Look at this."

I leaned over his shoulder—the shoulder *without* the parrot—and studied the screen. In a tall, narrow window, there was a long scroll of postings. I started reading.

"So?" I said. "It just looks like a bunch of dudes talking about the Big Air Games."

"Look at this one posted by 4567TME," he said, reading out loud. "'I hope you Xtreme sports nuts know how to dial 911.'"

I shrugged. "4567TME has a point. Extreme sports *are* dangerous. Most of those athletes wind up in the hospital sooner or later."

"Maybe," Frank admitted. "But it *could* be a threat. Maybe 4567TME plans to *put* those athletes in the hospital. And *sooner,* not later."

I rolled my eyes. "Man, you're making something out of nothing. I think you're just bummed out because we don't have a detailed mission—or even suspects. No smugglers to bust. No bank robbers to catch. I think you're afraid to just kick back and have fun . . . for once."

Frank sighed. "Maybe you're right," he said, logging off the computer.

"I know I'm right. This'll be like a vacation, man! So pack your bags and get ready to tear up the mega-ramps with your brother. Okay?"

Frank smiled. "Okay."

I turned around and started filling my backpack with clothes and socks and underwear. Frank got up from the desk and walked to the video game player. He pressed EJECT and pulled out the disk.

I stopped packing. "What is it, Frank?" I asked. "Why are you staring at that disk?"

Frank paused. "I don't know," he answered. "You're probably right about everything. But I wonder. If this mission is nothing but fun and games, why is it called 'Extreme Danger'?"

I didn't know what to say.

But Playback did.

"Danger! Danger! Danger!"

4.
Warning Signs

Call me paranoid. But I couldn't shake the feeling that there was more to this mission than met the eye.

Extreme danger.

The phrase reminded me of a road sign warning—sort of like FALLING ROCKS or SLIPPERY WHEN WET.

I really wanted to do a little more snooping around online—check out some other extreme sports Web sites—so I packed my laptop along with my clothes.

"Ready to roll?" I asked Joe. He strolled into my room with his backpack and motorcycle helmet.

"Dad said he'd drive us to the garage," he said.

"Did you fill him in on our mission?"

33

"No, not yet," Joe answered. "Prepare to be interrogated by the master."

My brother wasn't kidding. Our dad, Fenton Hardy, used to be one of the New York City Police Department's top investigators. He could wrangle a confession out of anyone—mobsters, counterfeiters, jewel thieves, and yes, even his own sons. But even though he'd had more than his share of danger, he still got nervous when he heard what we were up to.

"We probably shouldn't tell Dad about our little skydiving incident," I said to Joe.

"No way. He'd totally freak."

"Okay, so here's our story. We found the pirated DVDs and handed the evidence over to the police, who arrested Wings after the dive. No snags. No surprises. Got it?"

"Got it."

"Good."

I zipped up my backpack, grabbed my helmet, and followed Joe downstairs. Mom and Dad were sitting in the living room watching the six o'clock news on TV.

"Okay, we're ready to go, Dad," Joe announced.

Mom looked up and frowned. "Go where?" she asked.

Dad shifted nervously in his chair. "Honey, I,

um, told the boys they could take a little trip to Philadelphia for a few days," he told her.

"Oh, you did, did you?" she said. "And what, may I ask, is the purpose of this little trip?"

I thought fast. "We're studying the birth of American democracy in history class next fall," I lied. "Joe and I figured we could get a head start with an educational tour of Philadelphia."

"Oh, really?" Mom said, narrowing her eyes.

"Yeah," Joe jumped in. "You know, I've always wanted to see the Liberty Bell."

"Uh-huh," Mom responded with more than a hint of suspicion. "And I suppose your little trip has nothing to do with the Big Air Games, which happen to be in Philadelphia this week?"

She pointed to the TV set. A reporter was interviewing a group of extreme sports athletes while skateboarders zipped up and down a ramp in the background.

Clearly Mom had learned a few tricks from Dad.

"Well, you know—if we have time," I said, "we *might* check out a *few* of the Big Air events."

Mom nodded and sighed. "Okay, you can go," she said. "But promise me you won't get any crazy ideas about all this extreme sports stuff. I don't want you taking risks like that. I don't even want you to ride your motorcycles at night. It's too dangerous."

"Don't worry, Mom. It won't be dark for a couple more hours," Joe assured her.

"We'll be extra careful," I added.

Dad stood up and fetched his car keys from the entry hall. "If you want to make it to Philly by nightfall, we'd better get going, boys," he said.

Joe and I grabbed our stuff and headed for the front door. But we froze in our tracks when we heard a familiar voice behind us.

"Those boys aren't going anywhere."

We turned around to see Aunt Trudy standing in the dining room with two plates of food.

"That's right," she said. "Those boys aren't going anywhere until they finish their dinner. They're growing boys, and they need to eat."

"Wow, that's awfully sweet of you, Aunt Trudy," I said, trying to butter her up. "But we have to hurry off to Philadelphia now. You wouldn't want us to ride our motorcycles in the dark, would you?"

Aunt Trudy adjusted her glasses. "No, I guess not. But let me pack you a doggy bag. It'll just take a minute."

"We don't have a minute, Aunt Trudy," I explained. "We really have to go. Now."

She sighed. "All right, then," she said. "But what's the big rush? What's waiting for you in Philadelphia?"

"The Liberty Bell, Trudy," Mom chimed in. "The boys are going to learn that the bell cracked in 1753, the very first time it was rung. And the note it plays is E-flat."

Mom winked at Joe and me.

Pretty cool for a librarian.

But Aunt Trudy wasn't satisfied. "What about my VW?" she asked.

"I'll tell the guys at the garage to check it out," Dad volunteered.

Phew.

"Okay, but what about that bird?" said Aunt Trudy. "It doesn't even have a cage. It's going to poop all over the house."

I gave her my sweetest look. "Do you think you could take care of him while we're gone?" I asked with a smile. "It'll only be for a couple of days." I worked harder at my sweet smile.

Aunt Trudy melted. "Oh, all right," she gave in. "I'll feed him. But I won't clean up his messes!"

"Love you, Aunt Trudy," I said, giving her a peck on the cheek.

Joe and I hugged Mom and headed out the door. "Bye!"

"If you can remember, pick me up some Band-Aids!" Aunt Trudy shouted after us.

Once we were loaded into Dad's car, I let out a big sigh of relief. "Glad to get that over with," I whispered to Joe.

I'd spoken too soon.

"Okay, boys," said Dad, pulling out of the driveway. "Tell me all about your last mission."

Once again Joe and I were forced to tell some little white lies—and Dad was harder to fool than Mom and Aunt Trudy. Taking a deep breath, I gave Dad the watered-down version of our skydiving mission. He listened quietly, waiting until I was done.

Then he said, "That's an interesting story, Frank. But you left out the part about your pull cords being cut."

My jaw dropped open. "How did you—?"

"Lieutenant Jones is an old friend of mine," he explained. "We were on the police force together in New York. And he told me everything that happened. Unlike you."

I felt my face get warm. "Dad, we hate lying to you, but . . ."

"We didn't want you to freak out," said Joe.

Dad glanced at us through the rearview mirror. "Look, guys. When I left the force and started up

American Teens Against Crime, I knew it would involve risks. But I also knew that you boys can take care of yourselves . . . and each other."

Joe nudged me in the ribs. I nudged him back.

"I was always impressed with the amateur detective work you did a couple of years ago," Dad continued. "The cops at the station used to call you the Sherlock Brothers of Bayport. You solved some major crimes. Cases even the police couldn't crack. And you mixed with some major criminals. Sure, I was worried. But I couldn't be prouder."

I smiled. "Thanks, Dad."

"Yeah, thanks," said Joe.

Dad's expression changed. "But now . . . I don't know," he said, lowering his voice. "It's a tough world out there. Maybe it's too much to ask teenagers to go undercover. It's just too dangerous. And now that I'm semiretired, I can't keep a close eye on you boys."

"But Dad, we have the entire ATAC team looking out for us," I told him.

"Yeah, man, we're covered," said Joe.

Dad took a deep breath and let it out slowly. "I guess you're right," he said. "But you can't blame a guy for worrying about his kids. Especially when they're jumping out of planes and busting smugglers."

"That's what we live for!" said Joe.

Dad chuckled. "So tell me all about this new mission. What's up with the Big Air Games? Are the athletes using steroids, or bribing judges, or what?"

"I wish it was that specific," I said. Then Joe and I filled him in on the details.

"Basically they want us to keep an eye on the other teenagers," Joe explained.

"We're just undercover baby-sitters," I added with a sigh.

"Don't be so sure," said Dad. "The ATAC team wouldn't be sending you unless they detected something suspicious. Just stay on your guard. And have some fun . . . within limits. Remember my motto."

"Suspect *everyone*," Joe and I said at the same time.

"Good boys." Dad steered the car off the highway and pulled into the front lot of the Bayport Auto Garage. "Go get 'em," he said.

My brother and I hopped out and dashed into the garage. We were dying to see our bikes. Butch, the head mechanic, had promised to upgrade our motorcycles with some new parts.

"Yo, bros," Butch greeted us. "You prepared to be blown away?"

"Go ahead," said Joe. "Make my day."

The mustached mechanic waved us into the garage. "Feast your eyes on these babies," he said.

One word: *Wow.*

These were no ordinary motorcycles. These were total high-tech speed machines decked out with all the latest features! Polished chrome controls, high-grade leather seats, stainless steel exhaust pipes—the works—and they were customized with flaming red double Hs.

"This is *too much*!" Joe yelped. "This *kicks butt*!"

I couldn't believe my eyes. "What . . . ? How . . . ? Why did you do all this, Butch?" I said, stammering. "I mean, we just brought our bikes in for a tune-up."

Butch laughed and walked over to the motorcycles. "Check this out," he said, demonstrating the new features. "Hydraulic clutch. Optimized suspension. Fog lamps with flint protectors. Hazard warning flashers. Digital clock, CD player, and CB radio. Electric power socket for accessories."

"Dude! Stop! You're killing me!" Joe whooped out loud, faking a heart attack.

"But wait. That's not all," Butch went on. He flicked a switch, and a series of digital panels lit up on the dashboard. "Check it out, guys. Here you have your security tracking device and computerized navigation system."

"Unreal!" Joe hooted.

I stared in shock.

This was unbelievable.

Finally I managed to speak. "You weren't kidding when you said you'd upgrade our bikes, Butch. But the problem is, I don't know how we're going to pay for all this."

"Forget about it," said the mechanic. "It's taken care of." He nodded toward a man standing in the doorway.

"Dad!" Joe shouted. "You totally rock!"

"You boys deserve it," Dad said with a big grin. "Now saddle up and make your father proud."

Joe hooted and hopped on his bike. I looked my father in the eye. "You didn't have to do this," I said.

He shrugged. "I just thought you boys should have all the new safety features when you're chasing down bad guys."

I smiled. "Okay, cool. Thanks." Then I turned and tested out the new leather seat of my bike.

"Just do me one favor, Frank," Dad said when I reached for the ignition. "Don't take this new mission too lightly. They must have named it 'Extreme Danger' for a reason."

"That's what I told Joe."

"Well, be careful," said Dad.

Joe and I slipped our helmets over our heads and revved up our engines. Then, waving good-bye to Dad, we roared out of the parking lot and headed down the highway.

Joe was so happy he looked like he was going to self-destruct.

I glanced over my shoulder for one last look at Dad. He was standing in the middle of the lot, watching us ride off. Even from a block away, I could see the concern on his face.

A warning sign.

Unfortunately, I should have been paying attention to *other* signs—like the road signs in front of me.

Because I'd missed the turn for the interstate.

And Joe was nowhere in sight!

5.

Killer Wheels

Philadelphia, here we come!

Man, I was having a blast. With the new killer wheels beneath me and the open road in front of me, I was ready to take on the world—or, at least, tackle our latest mission.

There was just one problem: Where was Frank?

Turns out he'd fallen behind. But thanks to our new navigation systems, he was able to catch up with me on the next interstate ramp. Zooming up next to me, he grinned and gave me a thumbs-up.

All systems go.

We made good time. Weaving our way through the rush-hour traffic, we reached the outskirts of Philadelphia by eight o'clock. My motorcycle handled like a dream.

Heck, I could have kept riding all night long.

Minutes later we found the hotel and pulled our cycles into the parking garage. "Do I have to leave my bike here?" I asked Frank, turning off the engine. "Do you think they'll let me park it in my room? I could say it's my luggage."

"You could also say you're Elvis, but I don't think they'll go for it," said Frank. "Come on. Let's check in."

We gathered up our stuff and grabbed an elevator to the lobby. When the doors opened, we thought we'd come to the wrong place.

The joint was rocking!

It was a total zoo. Every inch of the hotel lobby was crawling with punked-out dudes and dudettes sporting Mohawks and Day-Glo dye jobs. Across the room, a gang of bikers in red leather knocked their helmets together and cheered. A pack of T-shirted skateboarders did railslides down the entry steps. A ponytailed trio of identical triplets zipped past us on Rollerblades.

"Hey, Frank," I said, nudging my brother. "If they can skate around in here, maybe I can ride my bike, too."

"Give it a rest, Joe."

Frank pointed me toward the reception desk. Zigzagging our way through the crowd, we walked up to the check-in sign—and found ourselves face-to-face with a bald-headed desk clerk who didn't look at all amused by the hotel's current clientele.

"May I help you, gentlemen?" he said with a tired sigh.

"I'll take care of this," Frank told me.

"Sure, knock yourself out."

My brother loved handling this sort of official business. Fine with me. It gave me a chance to scan the room and check out the action.

I turned around—and nearly knocked a girl over.

"Whoa! Sorry," I said, grabbing her wrist before she fell. "Are you okay?"

The girl looked up. "No problem. I'm okay."

She was more than okay. She was a total knockout—a brown-eyed beauty with jet black hair, ruby red lips, and a hot-pink skateboard tucked under her arm.

This mission was looking better all the time.

"I'm Joe. Joe Hardy." I extended my hand.

The girl slapped it and smiled. "I'm Jenna Cho. And I'm *so* embarrassed."

"Embarrassed? Why?" I asked.

She held up her skateboard and shrugged. "Well, it's like this. Twenty minutes ago I did a 540 air spin on the half-pipe and had no problem landing on my board. Then this dude bumps into me in a hotel lobby and I totally wipe out."

I laughed. "This dude sounds like a jerk," I said.

"No, not really," Jenna said with a wink. "In fact, he's kind of cute."

Nice.

"Are you competing in the games?" Jenna asked me.

"No, I'm just a fan," I said. "But I skateboard a little myself. I wish I'd brought mine with me."

"Well, if you want to borrow mine, I'll be practicing in FDR Park tomorrow," said Jenna. "All the Big Air boarders hang out there."

"Sure, I'll drop by," I said, even though I wasn't thrilled about riding a hot-pink skateboard.

"Jenna! Come on!" someone yelled across the lobby. I looked over to see a group of skateboarders in front of the elevators.

"Chill out! I'm coming!" Jenna yelled back at them. She threw her board on the floor and hopped on. "I'm in room 514," she whispered. "Call me if you want to hang." Then she skated away.

Excellent.

"Who was that?" asked Frank, coming up behind me.

"A beautiful girl who just gave me her room number," I bragged.

"Why was she whispering?"

"Probably because she didn't want *you* to hear it."

"Or maybe she has something to hide."

"Oh, come off it, Frank. Stop playing detective for two minutes and enjoy yourself."

My brother looked annoyed. "We're here on a mission, Joe," he said, lowering his voice. "We're supposed to be gathering information."

"Yes, and the best way to do that is by blending in and hanging out with the athletes," I replied. "And besides, I *did* get some information. Jenna told me that all the skateboarders practice in FDR Park."

Frank raised an eyebrow. "Okay, well, that's useful," he admitted. "Anyway, I have our room keys. Let's go."

We took the elevator up to our hotel room, unpacked our stuff—and suddenly realized we were starving.

"We should have taken Aunt Trudy's doggy bags when we had the chance," said Frank.

"Let's go out and grab a slice of pizza," I suggested. "We have the whole city of Philadelphia at our feet."

Frank agreed.

We left our room and went downstairs, passing through the circus in the lobby and heading for an exit. When we got outside, we were surprised to see that the sidewalks were just as crowded as the hotel.

"Man, the whole city is buzzing," said Frank, staring at all the extreme athletes and fans passing by.

I could tell he was trying to eavesdrop on their conversations—listening for anything suspicious. That was my brother. Always on the case.

We walked a few blocks, just enjoying the sights, until we stumbled on a small skateboard store. The place was a little run-down but seemed to carry all the latest boards and equipment. A sign above the door said OLLIE'S SKATE SHOP.

"Let's go in," said Frank. "We can ask the owner if he's heard any rumors about an attack."

I was starving, but I didn't feel like arguing with my brother. He was a man on a mission.

A little bell jingled when we opened the door and stepped inside. The place was packed with merchandise, but not many customers. There were just a few teenaged boys trying on helmets, and two girls looking at T-shirts.

"Hey! You boys!" a deep gravelly voice shouted from behind the counter.

Frank and I turned to see who was shouting. It was a middle-aged man with a bad sunburn, a walking cane, tattooed arms, and long blond hair tied in a ponytail. He looked kind of like an angry surfer.

Lucky for us, he was pointing at the other boys in the store. "Don't put those helmets on your greasy little heads unless you're serious about buying them," he barked.

"Oh, get over yourself, dude," one of the boys shot back. "I don't care if you *were* the national champion. That was years ago. Right now, you're a knobby-kneed has-been!"

The ponytailed man fixed his cold blue eyes on the boys—then slowly reached under the counter. "Get out of my store," he snarled. "Now."

Nobody moved for a moment or two. Then the boys put down the helmets and walked out of the store. "Loser," one of them mumbled as the door closed with a jingle.

Frank tapped my arm, then nodded at a handwritten sign next to the register. It said, AS AN AMERICAN CITIZEN, I FULLY EXERCISE MY RIGHT TO BEAR ARMS. SHOPLIFTERS: BEWARE.

I glanced back at Frank. He raised his eyebrows and tilted his head toward a bulletin board.

I turned and looked. The board was covered with photos of Ollie looking young and fit—and soaring through the air on a skateboard. There were newspaper clippings, too, with headlines like OLLIE PETERSON: NATIONAL SKATEBOARD CHAMP 1986 and OLLIE WINS AGAIN! I had to squint to read the small clipping on the bottom: SKATEBOARD LEGEND TAKES A FALL.

"What are you boys looking for?" Ollie grunted, slamming his cane down on the counter.

I tried to think fast. "I need a new skateboard," I answered. "Something top-of-the-line."

Ollie growled and lowered his cane, then limped toward a large skateboard display. "Over here, kid," he said. "I got all the latest models."

Why not buy one? That way I wouldn't have to share Jenna's tomorrow.

It took only about three minutes for Ollie to convince me to buy a brand-new THX-720 with red flame detailing. And it matched my motorcycle!

Frank, in the meantime, was studying the articles on the bulletin board—gathering information, as usual.

As Ollie rang up my purchase, one of the girls walked up to the counter and said, "Excuse me? Mister? Do you have any T-shirts for the Big Air Games?"

Wrong question.

Ollie almost threw a fit. "Big Air *Heads* is more

SUSPECT PROFILE

<u>Name:</u> Owen Peterson, aka "Ollie"

<u>Hometown:</u> San Diego, CA

<u>Physical description:</u> 40 years old, 5'11", 170 pounds, shoulder-length blond hair, blue eyes, walks with limp, carries cane, dragon tattoos on forearms

<u>Occupation:</u> Owner/operator of Ollie's Skate Shop in downtown Philadelphia

<u>Background:</u> Former professional skateboarder (career ended after accidental injury in 1990)

<u>Suspicious behavior:</u> Threatened customers, reached for (alleged) gun under store counter, talked about replacing skateboard bearings with nitroglycerin

<u>Suspected of:</u> Attempted sabotage

<u>Possible motives:</u> Revenge against Big Air Games (business dispute), personal resentment

like it!" he snapped. "Those big-business money-grubbers won't allow me to set up a stand outside the stadium. So, fat chance I'll fill their greedy pockets by selling their ugly shirts."

The girl blinked her eyes. "So that's a no?" she asked.

"YES, IT'S A NO!" he boomed.

The girl shrugged and left the store with her friend.

A few seconds later Ollie calmed down enough to take my money and complete my purchase.

Frank strolled over to the counter. "I guess those Big Air Games are a big deal, huh?" he said to Ollie.

Ollie rolled his eyes. "A big pain," he sneered. "The whole city is tied in knots, with all the traffic and the cops everywhere."

"Well, an event that big must attract a lot of weirdos," said Frank. "Maybe even terrorists. Someone told me they heard a rumor that someone was going to sabotage the games."

Ollie laughed. "That would be fine with me," he growled. "I even know how they could do it."

"Oh, really?" said Frank, leaning over the counter. "How?"

Ollie grabbed a skateboard off the display and flipped it over. "See the axis of the wheel here?" he said, giving it a spin. "That's where the ball bearings usually go. But some of these new models use liquid bearings. No balls, just liquid. Understand?"

Frank and I nodded.

"Well, imagine this," Ollie continued. "What if

someone replaced the liquid with an explosive like nitroglycerin? Think about it. The faster the skater goes, the hotter the nitro gets. Faster and hotter, faster and hotter, until . . . *KA-BOOM!* I think you get the picture."

Yes, we got the picture.

And it wasn't very pretty.

Talk about killer wheels.

I grabbed my new skateboard and nudged my brother. "Come on, Frank. We better get going. It's late."

My brother agreed. "Bye, Ollie," he said as we left the store. "It was nice talking to you."

Yeah, I thought. *It's always nice to talk to a crazy washed-up skateboarder who wants to blow people up.*

6.

Attacked!

Joe and I didn't get to eat until ten o'clock at night. *(My fault, because it was my idea to go inside Ollie's Skate Shop.)*

And we didn't get to sleep until one o'clock in the morning. *(Joe's fault, because it was his idea to call up Jenna Cho when we returned to the hotel.)*

Anyway, Jenna convinced my brother that we should skip the pregame events in the morning. The official opening ceremonies would be held the following day. She suggested we sleep in, grab a late breakfast, then meet her in the park with the other skaters.

Sounded good to me. I was exhausted.

After a full day of skydiving, motorcycle-riding,

skateboard-shopping, a whole pizza at ten o'clock—and listening to Joe yammer on with his new girlfriend—who could blame me for being tired?

Ah, sleep.

"Wake up!" said Joe, hitting me with a pillow. "Are you going to sleep all day? Move your lazy butt!"

I rubbed my eyes and looked at the clock radio.

Nine forty-five?

I think it was the first time in history that Joe woke up before I did. "Breakfast," I mumbled sleepily.

"No time for that," said Joe, tossing me a pair of shorts and a shirt. "We promised to meet Jenna. Move it."

I crawled out of bed, hopped in the shower, and got dressed as quickly as I could. Joe insisted that we ride our cycles to the park.

"We don't want to be late," he said, adding, "and girls dig the bikes."

About twenty minutes later, we arrived at FDR Park. Jenna Cho was waiting with her pink skateboard at the entrance.

"Yo, dudes!" She greeted us with a big smile and a thumbs-up. "Awesome set of wheels! I'm impressed."

"Told you so," Joe whispered to me. Then he

flashed a smile at his new friend. "How's it going, Jenna?"

Jenna swung her skateboard like a baseball bat. "It's going, it's going, it's gone!" she said, laughing. "Come on, park your bikes so we can grab some cheese steaks."

"Philly cheese steaks?" I asked. "For breakfast?"

Joe swatted my arm. "This is my brother," he explained to Jenna. "Frank is the logical Hardy."

"Yeah, and Joe is *hardly* logical," I added.

After the introduction we found a spot to park our bikes and ordered three cheese steaks at a nearby stand.

"Wow," I said, taking a bite. "This is incredible."

Jenna nodded. "Now you know why they're world famous."

We strolled through the park, chomping on our cheese steaks, while Jenna showed us the sights. "I'm taking you guys to a skatepark underneath the overpass," she said. "It was built by the city. All the cool Philly kids skate there."

"Can't wait," Joe said, waving the new skateboard he'd bought at Ollie's.

"Where's your board, Frank?" asked Jenna.

I shrugged. "With pros like you around, I didn't want to risk looking like a dork."

"Too late for that," my brother teased.

I decided to change the subject. Now was my chance to ask about the rumors of a possible attack. "Speaking of risks," I started off, "someone told me they saw some threats posted on one of the extreme Web sites. Some people even think someone plans to sabotage the games. You heard anything, Jenna?"

Jenna thought about it, then said, "I don't know, just the usual rivalries. Competition can get pretty fierce. There's a lot of money at stake."

"There is?" I asked.

"Well, the top prizes are ten thousand dollars," she said. "And if you win the nationals, you could land a million-dollar endorsement deal from the sports gear companies."

Definitely a motive for sabotaging your opponent, I thought.

We were almost in the middle of the park. A few kids on skateboards and motocross bikes whizzed past us. "The skatepark is over there," Jenna said, pointing past some trees.

Suddenly a loud siren blasted right behind us.

"Look out!" Joe yelled.

We jumped out of the way as a white EMT ambulance barreled past us with its lights flashing.

"It's heading for the skatepark!" Jenna shouted. "Maybe there's been an accident!"

"Let's go," I said, slapping my brother's shoulder.

The three of us dashed after the ambulance, pushing past dozens of gawking skaters and bikers. The siren stopped blaring. The vehicle pulled to a halt in front of a graffiti-covered ramp under the highway overpass. We rushed over to the center of the action.

A muscular dark-haired boy lay on the concrete next to his skateboard. "It hurts! It hurts!" he howled in pain.

"I know that boy," Jenna whispered to Frank and me. "That's Gongado Lopez. He's from New York City, and everyone says he's a sure thing for a gold medal this year."

Not anymore.

A tall skinny paramedic applied bandages to the boy's knees and shouted over his shoulder, "Jack! I need some help here!"

A short stocky technician jumped out of the ambulance with a small case of supplies. I watched the two men do their job and I checked out the ID badges on their chests.

The short guy was named Jack Horowitz, and the tall skinny guy was Carter Bean. Carter seemed to be the more experienced of the two. He filled a hypodermic needle and gave Gongado a shot of painkiller in about fifteen seconds flat.

"Gongado!" a high-pitched voice cried out. "Gongado! What did that dirtbag do to you?"

A short frizzy-haired young woman pushed past us and rushed toward the stricken boy. Carter blocked her with his arm. "Stay back, miss," he said firmly. "Let us do our jobs."

The girl backed off but kept talking. "Gongado! Sweetie! What happened? Tell me!"

Gongado blinked his eyes. Obviously the painkillers were kicking in, but he was able to talk. "Baby, I was attacked! Somebody jumped me and knocked me over and whacked me in the knees with my own skateboard."

The girl burst into tears. "Was it him?" she asked. "Was it Eddie?"

Gongado shook his head. "I don't know. I didn't see his face." Then he closed his eyes and passed out.

A man with a camera stepped forward. "Did anyone see anything?" he shouted into the crowd.

Nobody said anything.

"Are you a police officer?" Carter asked the man.

"No, I'm a reporter for the *Philadelphia Freedom Press,*" he told the paramedic. "I was just walking through the park when I heard your siren. Do you mind posing for a picture? Just crouch over the victim and try to look concerned."

"I *am* concerned," Carter said calmly. He turned to help his coworker lift the boy onto a stretcher and into the ambulance.

The reporter snapped away with his camera. Even after the ambulance drove off, he kept pursuing the story. But instead of taking pictures, he interviewed half the kids in the crowd.

After a while, the reporter went away—and the scene returned to normal. The skateboarders practiced their kickies and heelies while the bikers hurtled over ramps. Jenna, Joe, and I found a spot under a nearby tree.

"Do you know that girl? Gongado's girlfriend?" I asked Jenna.

"I don't know her personally," she said, "but I know *about* her. Her name's Annette, and she only dates the hottest skateboarders in town. She used to go out with Eddie Mundy . . . until Gongado beat him in the last regional contest. Now she goes out with Gongado."

"Eddie Mundy," I said. "Annette mentioned Eddie's name. So she thinks Eddie attacked Gongado?"

"Of course she does," said Jenna. "Gongado stole Eddie's title. Then he stole Eddie's girl. You do the math."

"What's this Eddie guy like?" I asked.

Jenna pointed across the park. "That's him over there. In the red bandanna." She poked my brother's arm. "Come on, Joe. Want to try out the vert ramp?"

Joe and Jenna ran off with their skateboards.

And me? I decided to have a little talk with Eddie Mundy.

"Hey, man," I said, approaching him during a break. "I hear you're the best skateboarder in town."

Eddie sat down on his board and looked up at me suspiciously. "Who told you that?" he asked. He was lean, lanky—and a little scary-looking, I had to admit.

"Some of the other athletes said you were the best," I said, nodding at the other skateboarders.

Eddie shrugged. "I *used* to be the best," he grunted. "Until Gongado Lopez snatched my title away."

"Well, they just took Lopez away in an ambulance," I said. "His knees are all busted up. So I guess he's out of the contest now."

"Yeah," said Eddie, squinting his eyes. "So I guess that makes *me* the best." He let out a little laugh.

"Did you and Gongado get along?" I asked.

Eddie didn't answer. He just stared at me. "Why do you ask so many questions, man?"

"I'm writing an article on the Big Air Games for my school paper," I lied.

"Well, watch your back," said Eddie. "It's dangerous to ask too many questions. *Extremely* dangerous."

He gave me a hard look. I figured I was pushing my luck, so I simply said thanks and good-bye.

SUSPECT PROFILE

<u>Name:</u> Edward Mundy, aka "Eddie"

<u>Physical description:</u> 18 years old, 6'1", 180 pounds, brown hair, green eyes, wears red bandanna

<u>Hometown:</u> Philadelphia, PA

<u>Occupation:</u> Hardware store clerk, amateur skateboarder

<u>Background:</u> Former titleholder in regional skateboard contests, currently competing in Big Air Games

<u>Suspicious behavior:</u> Laughed about Gongado Lopez's attack and leg injuries, referred to Frank's questioning as "extremely dangerous"

<u>Suspected of:</u> Assault and battery

<u>Possible motives:</u> Professional revenge (Lopez stole his title), romantic triangle (Lopez stole his girl)

I walked around the skateboard park looking for Joe. I wanted to get him up to speed.

We had another suspect.

A few minutes later I managed to drag Joe away from the concrete ramps—and away from Jenna. She said she needed to practice for her upcoming event, so my brother and I headed off on our own.

I waited until we were about a hundred yards away from the skatepark—safely out of everyone's earshot—before I told Joe about my talk with Eddie Mundy.

"Man!" Joe said, after hearing my story. "That dude is *so* guilty."

"We don't know that for a fact," I pointed out. "Sure, Eddie has the motives—and the attitude—to commit a crime like that. But there's no real evidence."

"But come on," Joe argued. "How else do you explain his comment about your 'dangerous' questions?"

I scratched my head. "I don't know," I said. "It's definitely suspicious. And we definitely should keep an eye on Eddie Mundy."

"So that's it?" Joe said, throwing his hands up. "We just keep an eye on the guy? We don't turn him in to the cops?"

"No. Not yet."

Joe stopped walking. "But Frank," he persisted. "What if Eddie Mundy hurts someone else?"

I thought long and hard about my brother's question. But I never got the chance to answer him.

Because somebody started screaming.

7.

Blood on the Half-Pipe

Man! What a scream!

Frank and I stood still and listened.

There it was again!

I don't know what freaked me out more: the fact that the scream came from the skateboard park, or that it sounded like Jenna doing the screaming. I took off like a bolt of lightning, sprinting as fast as I could toward the concrete overpass. Frank's footsteps echoed behind me. Other skaters and bikers were dashing toward the half-pipes—but I outran them all.

A group of people were crowded around one of the pipes. I spotted a dark-haired girl hunched down in the middle of the circle.

"Jenna!" I yelled, pushing past the onlookers.

Jenna sat on the curve of the ramp, leaning over the lifeless body of a curly-haired boy.

I dropped to my knees beside her. "What happened? Is he okay?"

Jenna looked up at me, her eyes filled with tears. "I don't know," she said. "We were practicing our air jumps, and Jeb just collapsed in front of me. Then my skateboard slammed into his head. I tried to stop, but . . ."

I carefully examined the boy's scalp, parting the locks of his curly hair. "I don't see any head wounds," I said. "And he's still breathing. Somebody call 911!"

"I already did," said Frank, shoving his cell phone back in his pocket and stooping down next to us. He looked at Jenna. "Who is he? Do you know him?"

Jenna nodded. "Jeb Green. He's an old friend of mine from California. An amazing skateboarder. He knows how to take a fall. But this time . . . it was weird . . . he fell with a bang."

"A bang?" I said, glancing at Frank.

"It's all my fault," Jenna sobbed quietly. "I tried to stop before I ran into him, but my skateboard shot out from under me. I might have given him a concussion."

"I don't think your skateboard did this," I said,

pointing to the upper curve of the ramp. "There's blood on the half-pipe."

"And here, too," Frank added. "In the middle of the guy's chest."

We quickly unbuttoned the boy's shirt—and exposed a small bullet hole in his skin.

"Jeb was shot!" Jenna gasped.

The crowd started buzzing like flies. Some of them took off running, while others moved in for a closer look. One man kept saying, "Excuse me, pardon me, coming through," until he pushed his way in.

It was the reporter from the *Philadelphia Freedom Press*.

"So what happened here?" he asked. "Any eye-witnesses?"

Jenna started to speak, but I stopped her.

There was something about this guy I didn't like. Maybe it was the way he hoisted up his camera and started snapping away whenever people got hurt.

"Hey, buddy," I said. "This boy might be dying here. Give the camera a rest."

The reporter scoffed. "Are you kidding? This is front page material."

I felt like punching the guy. But Frank had a better idea. He simply stood up—and blocked the reporter's view.

In the distance a siren began to wail.

"Okay, everybody move out of the way!" Frank yelled to the crowd. "Make room for the ambulance! Come on, guys! Move it!"

Slowly the kids backed away, leaving space for the approaching EMT van.

Soon the ambulance came to a halt in front of the ramp. The doors flew open and out stepped Carter and Jack—the same paramedics who'd treated Gongado Lopez about an hour before.

"Busy day," I said, stepping out of their way.

"Not really," replied Carter. "Accidents happen every day."

"This wasn't an accident," Frank told him.

"Oh, I see," said the thin paramedic, examining Jeb's chest wound.

"Is he . . . is he going to live?" Jenna asked.

"Well, the hole is too small for a regular bullet," Carter said. "This looks like it was made by a pellet gun." He inspected the wound further. "Yes, here it is, lodged in his sternum."

Jenna sucked in her breath. "But is he . . . ?"

"Yes, he's going to live," the paramedic added.

The crowd of onlookers cheered. Even the reporter from the *Freedom Press* looked happy—although he didn't stop taking pictures for a single second.

The EMT guys ignored all the attention. They were completely committed to their work. I was amazed at how fast and efficient they were. In only minutes Carter and Jack had the boy safely strapped onto a stretcher and hooked up to an IV drip.

I put my arm around Jenna's shoulder. "Jeb's going to be okay," I told her. "These guys know what they're doing."

Jack, the shorter paramedic, climbed into the driver's seat and revved the engine. Carter stayed in the back with the patient. Just before the ambulance pulled away, Carter peered out the rear window and gave the skateboarders a thumbs-up.

Everybody cheered.

"Beautiful! Just beautiful!" the reporter exclaimed, capturing the whole scene with his camera. Then he pulled a handheld tape recorder from his pocket and started asking people questions.

I looked down at Jenna. She looked pretty shell-shocked. "Maybe you should sit down for a minute," I suggested.

"There's a bench over there," Frank said, pointing.

The three of us walked over and sat down. Hidden away beneath a big shady tree, the bench offered a perfect view of the skateboard park. Nobody was skating or riding. Everyone was milling about and talking.

We didn't talk for a while—just watched the others from a distance.

Finally Jenna spoke. "Why would anyone want to shoot Jeb? It doesn't make any sense." She kicked an empty soda can back and forth between her feet.

I glanced at Frank.

I knew he was *dying* to ask Jenna some questions, but he didn't say a word.

"I just don't get it," she said softly. "Everybody loves Jeb. He's one of those sunny California guys. Always happy, always smiling. No enemies, no rivals. He's just a cool, laid-back kind of guy. I wish you two could meet him."

"Maybe Frank and I can visit him at the hospital," I said.

"Would you?" she said, her eyes lighting up. "That would mean a lot to me. Maybe I should skip practice and go with you."

"I bet Jeb would want you to practice and kick butt on the ramps tomorrow. Don't you think?" I asked.

She nodded. "Yeah, you're right. But tell him that I'm pulling for him, and I'll try to visit him tonight."

I gave her a big hug. "Go practice," I said.

Jenna smiled and stretched. Then she threw

down her board and skated off toward the ramps.

I couldn't take my eyes off of her, for two reasons.

One, I was falling for her.

Two, I was worried about her.

"The shooter is still out there, Frank," I said. "He could be watching right now . . . and waiting to pull the trigger again."

"Maybe not," said Frank. "Here comes Eddie Mundy."

Warning bells went off in my head.

Eddie skated toward us with a red bandanna on his head, a backpack on his shoulder, and a hot dog in his mouth. He screeched to a stop in front of our bench.

"Hey! Mr. School Newspaper Reporter!" he barked at Frank. "What did I miss? What was up with the ambulance in the skatepark again?"

As if you don't know, I thought.

"There was another accident," Frank told the skater. "Jeb Green ran into a bullet."

Eddie stopped chewing his hot dog. "You're kidding me," he said.

"Why would I kid? I'm Mr. School Newspaper Reporter, remember?"

"Dude, that's pretty heavy-duty news," said Eddie, shaking his head. "Is Jeb dead?"

"No, he's in the hospital," Frank answered. "Seems he was shot with a pellet gun. You know, the small kind you could probably fit in a backpack."

Eddie glanced at the pack on his shoulder then smiled. "Hey, man. I wasn't even here, so don't even think it." He took another bite of his hot dog.

I couldn't take this guy another minute.

"So where were you, Eddie?" I asked.

He smirked at me. "I was grabbing a dog. See?" He opened his mouth and showed us the chewed-up food.

"Where did you buy it?" Frank asked.

Eddie shrugged. "A vendor."

"Which vendor?"

"Dude, how do I know? There are like a hundred vendors in this park!" He laughed—until he saw the look on our faces. "You guys are serious, aren't you? You really think I'm picking off the other skateboarders. Why? You think it's the only way I can win a medal? Give me a break, man!"

Eddie hopped on his board and skated away.

I looked at Frank. "I think I'm going to hang around the skatepark for a little bit. I don't like the idea of Jenna practicing while that creep is around."

Frank nodded. "Here's an idea. I'll go question

some of the hot dog vendors in the area, see if Eddie was really there during the shooting. Meet me at the park entrance in about a half hour. Cool?"

"Cool."

We parted ways. I headed into the skatepark and found a spot under the overpass where I could keep an eye on both Jenna and Eddie. After a while my fears started to fade. Everything seemed back to normal.

But it had seemed normal right before the attacks.

"Hey, you. Kid," someone said to me.

I turned my head and groaned. It was the reporter from the *Philadelphia Freedom Press*. He had his tape recorder in one hand and his camera in the other.

"What do you want?" I asked him.

"You were here for both of the accidents," he said.

"Yeah, so? So were you."

"So what's your story, kid?" he asked. "You a skateboard freak? Would you kill to win the Big Air Games?"

I shot him a dirty look. "How do I know you're really a reporter?"

He pulled out a wallet and showed me his press

ID. I glanced at his grainy face shot and credentials: Maxwell Monroe, journalist/photographer, *Philadelphia Freedom Press.*

"Nice picture, Max," I said. "So why do you like taking pictures of violent crimes? What do you get out of it?"

"A Pulitzer Prize for journalism if I'm lucky," he answered, chuckling. "Maybe I'll stumble onto another attack today. It's crazy. Two teen assaults at the same place on the same day? And I happen to be right here to catch it all on camera? I mean, what are the chances of that?"

Yes, I thought. *What* are *the chances of that?*

"I tell you, most reporters would kill for this kind of story," Max went on. "I can see the headlines now. 'Big Crimes at Big Air Games! An exclusive report by Maxwell Monroe.' I'll be famous."

"Sure you will, Max," I said, slowly backing away. The guy was creeping me out.

"Well, kid, I have to get back to the office if I want to make my deadline." He slipped his little tape recorder into the inside pocket of his jacket.

That's when I noticed something: He was wearing a gun holster.

"Good luck with the games, son! Break a leg!"

Monroe turned and walked away, laughing to himself.

I turned my attention back to the ramps. Eddie Mundy was leaving the park with a group of friends. Seemed safe to leave Jenna.

I watched her do an amazing jump, said good-bye, and headed off to meet Frank at the park

SUSPECT PROFILE

Name: Maxwell Monroe

Hometown: Philadelphia, PA

Physical description: 48 years old, 6'2", 200 pounds, balding, brown eyes, glasses

Occupation: Journalist/photographer, Philadelphia Freedom Press

Background: Graduate of Farmdale Community College, former fact-checker for Weekly World News

Suspicious behavior: Just happened to "stumble" onto two crime scenes, harassed victims with camera, joked about possibility of more attacks

Suspected of: Assault, battery, attempted homicide with firearm, journalistic fraud

Possible motives: Pulitzer Prize, fame, fortune

entrance. I couldn't wait to give him the latest news.

If my suspicions were correct, tomorrow's headline just might read: LOCAL REPORTER WILLING TO KILL FOR GOOD STORY.

8.

Dead on Arrival

The emergency room at Pennsylvania Hospital was crowded, noisy, and hectic. The patients with the most severe injuries were wheeled past us on gurneys. Others had to wait in the seating area until a nurse at the desk shouted their names.

I shifted back and forth on the hard vinyl chair and tried to sort through the clues and suspects in my head. But it was hard to concentrate with all the moaning and groaning in the room. The patients were losing their patience. And so was I.

My brother wouldn't shut up about Maxwell Monroe.

"I'm telling you, Frank. That newspaper guy is a

total freak," Joe yammered on. "He'd do anything to get a good story."

"I don't know, Joe," I said. "It seems pretty far-fetched."

"But he was *there,* dude, for *both* attacks."

"So were we," I pointed out. "So were a lot of people."

"But what about his gun?"

"You didn't see a gun. You saw a shoulder holster. Maybe it was just the guy's camera strap."

"Maybe," Joe said, standing up and stretching his legs. "But maybe not."

It was hard to take Joe seriously. He was holding a bouquet of fresh daisies.

"Okay," I said. "I'll add his name to our suspect list. Let's see now. We have Maxwell Monroe, Ollie Peterson, Eddie Mundy . . . and every skateboarder competing in the games. That really narrows it down."

Joe sighed and rubbed his eyes.

"Hardy! HARDY!"

The desk nurse shouted out our names like an army drill sergeant. Joe and I rushed over to the desk.

"You can see Jebediah Green now," the nurse informed us. "They just moved him to room 418."

We left the emergency waiting room and headed

for the elevators. On the fourth floor, another nurse pointed us toward Jeb's room. I knocked lightly before we entered.

"Come in," said a gravelly voice.

My brother and I entered the room. Jeb was laid out in the hospital bed with a big gauze patch taped to his chest and an IV drip stuck in his arm.

Joe held out the bouquet of daisies. "These are from Jenna," he said. "We're friends of hers."

Jeb smiled weakly. "Thanks, dude."

"She wanted to come, but we told her you'd probably want her to stay and practice."

"Definitely." He looked a little woozy—but surprisingly strong, especially considering he'd just been shot in the chest with a pellet gun.

"I'm Frank Hardy," I said, shaking his hand. "This is my brother Joe. How are you feeling?"

"Beats me," he said with a goofy grin. "I got so many painkillers in me, I don't feel a thing. But they tell me I'm going to live."

Joe set the flowers on a table and pulled up a chair. "My brother and I are trying to figure this thing out, Jeb."

"You and half the cops in Philly," said Jeb. "Those guys asked me like, a zillion questions down in the emergency room."

"Mind if we ask a few more?" I said.

"Sure. Why not? Who's counting? But first let me tell you what I already told the cops. No, I don't have any enemies—none that I can think of, at least. No, I can't think of any reason why someone would go after both Lopez and myself. And no, I'm not one of the top competitors this year—so it's pointless to take me out of the games."

I nodded and sighed. "Thanks, Jeb. You just answered most of my questions."

"The cops were pretty thorough," he said.

I was stumped. And, judging by the look on my brother's face, so was Joe.

Then I thought of something.

"I have another question for you, Jeb."

"Shoot," he said, smiling.

I laughed at his word choice, then asked my question. "What can you tell me about Ollie Peterson? The owner of Ollie's Skate Shop?"

Just then the door swung open—and in walked the tall skinny paramedic who had treated Jeb in the park.

"Hello, Jeb," the man said, smiling. "I was told you can see visitors now." He glanced at Joe and me.

"No problem, dude," said Jeb. "Join the party."

The paramedic introduced himself. "I'm Carter Bean. You probably don't remember me, but I'm one of the emergency medical guys who picked you up at the park."

"Thanks, man. You saved my life," said Jeb, shaking his hand. "These are friends of mine, Frank and Joe Hardy. They're in town for the Big Air Games."

"We're also fans of your work," Joe told Carter. "We saw you handle both of those emergencies today in the park. You're a real pro."

Carter nodded. "Thanks. It's always nice to be appreciated." He looked at Jeb. "So how are you doing? Did they patch you up good?"

"Check it out," Jeb answered.

Carter pulled away the bandage and examined the wound. "Nice job," he said. "That'll heal up before you know it. Good thing the gunman must have been standing far away. If he had fired at a closer range, you'd have been DOA."

"What's that mean?" asked Jeb.

"Dead on arrival," Carter explained.

"How far away would you say the shooter was?" I asked.

Carter scratched his head. "Well, you'd have to ask a forensic expert, but I would guess a couple hundred feet, at least."

I made a mental note of it. Maybe it was a clue. Maybe not.

After a few minutes of chitchat, the paramedic announced that his lunch break was over. As soon as he left the room, I asked Jeb again about Ollie Peterson.

"What can I say, man? Ollie is Ollie," Jeb explained. "Everybody knows him and everybody hates him. But he's got the best skateboard shop in town. He really knows his stuff. Ollie was a former champ, you know. He was the hottest thing on wheels back in the eighties. He had a huge career ahead of him."

"So what happened?" I asked.

"Two things," said Jeb. "First, he claims he invented the 'ollie'—the move you make by smacking your foot down on the back of the board. Everybody knew that Rodney Mullen came up with it, though. He's a legend among skateboarders. Ollie was just a big joke, especially after he insisted that everyone call him Ollie. His real name is Owen."

"Okay. What's the second thing?"

"The accident," said Jeb. "It happened in 1990, at the peak of his career, in the FDR skatepark. Ollie was really pushing himself. He flew about ten feet in the air and slammed down knee-first on the edge of the half-pipe. He's lucky he can walk at all."

We thanked Jeb for the information. He asked

us to give Jenna a message—"Go for the gold, baby"—and gave us the peace sign. Then Joe and I exited the hospital, hopped on our motorcycles, and returned to the hotel.

"Man, I need a shower!" Joe said when we got back to our room. "I'm drenched in sweat." He peeled off his shirt and headed for the bathroom.

I decided to plug in my laptop and check out a few Web sites. Maybe people were chatting about the attacks this morning. I logged in, did a quick search, and found the official chat rooms of the Big Air Games.

Bingo.

The chat rooms were packed. Everybody was typing in their theories on the skateboard assaults. Some blamed terrorists. Others thought it was the work of motocross bikers. But nobody suggested anything that made any sense.

I was about to give up when something caught my eye.

It was one little message, posted among all the oddball conspiracy theories.

It said, "I told you this was going to happen. I warned you."

It was posted by 4567TME—the same person who had posted the strange warning to "Xtreme sports nuts."

I knew it! That message I read yesterday was a threat!

I scanned the rest of the chat list, scrolling down to see if 4567TME had posted anything else.

Nothing—just that one message.

But what a message.

Joe stepped out of the bathroom drying his hair with a towel.

"Joe. Come look at this," I said.

Joe leaned over the laptop and read the message. "We have to tell the police," he said. "Maybe they can trace the source of the message through the Web site."

"Not if the message was bounced there," I said. "It could take days, even weeks, to track it down."

"We don't have that much time. The games start tomorrow."

"I know," I said, reaching for my cell phone and dialing 411. I asked for the number of Ollie's Skate Shop.

"What are you doing?" said Joe.

I shushed him, then dialed the number. It rang.

"Yeah? What do you want?" Ollie's gruff voice snarled over the line.

"What are your store hours?" I asked.

"Noon to ten."

"Noon?" I said. "That seems pretty late to open a store."

"Who asked *you*?" he snapped back. "It's *my* store and I'll do whatever I want." He hung up.

I looked at Joe. "Ollie doesn't open his store until noon," I explained. "Which means he wasn't working this morning. He could have been at the park."

Joe brought up another piece of evidence. "The paramedic said the pellet gun was fired from several hundred feet away. So it wasn't one of the skateboarders who did it. They were all hanging around the ramps."

"But Eddie Mundy was buying a hot dog," I pointed out. "The vendors are several hundred feet away."

Joe shook his head. "I don't know, man. Eddie looked pretty bummed out when you told him about Jeb. I really think Ollie is the prime suspect here."

I had to agree. "He's bitter about his career. He hates the Big Air Games. He dreams up ways to sabotage skateboards."

"And he has a gun under his counter," Joe added.

"Ding, ding, ding!" I said. "It looks like we have a winner, folks."

"Definitely," Joe agreed. "Ollie's our man. So

what do we do now? Are we ready to turn him in?"

I shook my head. "We still don't have enough evidence to convict the guy."

Joe groaned. "You and your evidence." He flopped down on his bed. "So what do you suggest, Mr. Law and Order?"

"I think we should pay Ollie another visit," I said. "Let's see how he's taking the news about the skateboard attacks."

Five minutes later we left the hotel and walked the three blocks to Ollie's street.

Joe was getting more excited with every step.

"We have to nail that guy," he said under his breath. "He's so guilty I can smell it."

I think Joe was looking forward to some sort of big showdown—the kind you see in the movies. Ollie certainly had what it takes to be a big-screen villain. Even with his cane and his limp, he'd probably put up a good fight.

Be prepared for anything, I told myself.

Even so, I was totally shocked when Joe and I turned the corner.

Ollie's shop was surrounded by police cars and fenced off with yellow tape. The place was crawling with cops. Behind them an ambulance flashed its lights and blared its siren, then drove off down the street.

Joe and I pushed our way up to the police line. "What's going on? What happened?" Joe asked the officers.

Nobody would talk.

"I'll tell you what happened," said someone behind us.

Joe and I spun around.

It was Maxwell Monroe, the reporter from the *Philadelphia Freedom Press.*

"Ollie's been murdered," he said.

9.
Who Is Mr. X?

Ollie? Murdered?

I couldn't believe what I was hearing. Our prime suspect had just become the latest victim.

"How did it happen?" Frank asked the reporter.

"He was poisoned," Max told us. "I overheard the cops talking. They think someone slipped something into Ollie's coffee. They're sending a sample off to the lab to be tested."

Ollie? Murdered? I kept thinking. *Who would want to murder Ollie?*

Then I remembered the way he snapped at those customers in his shop last night. Ollie may have owned the best skateboard shop in Philly, but he certainly seemed to have a lot of enemies. According to Jeb, everybody hated the guy.

But did they hate him enough to kill him?

Max raised his camera and snapped more shots of the crime scene. "Mr. X strikes again," he said.

"Who's Mr. X?" I asked.

"Haven't you seen the evening edition of the *Freedom Press*?"

"No. It's only two o'clock now."

"We went to press early today. Had to beat the other papers with our scoop," Max explained. "Anyway, the cover story is by yours truly. Photos, exclusive interviews . . . all mine! Even Mr. X was my idea."

"Phantom of the Big Air Games," Frank muttered.

Max looked at Frank. "Yeah, I came up with that, but . . . I thought you hadn't seen the evening edition yet."

Frank pointed to the crime scene. Lying in the doorway of Ollie's shop was a crumpled copy of the *Freedom Press*. The headline read, WHO IS MR. X? PHANTOM OF THE BIG AIR GAMES ATTACKS XTREME ATHLETES IN PARK.

"Mr. X. Xtreme sports. Get it?" said Max.

"We get it," I said.

"Better yet, buy it," the reporter added. "My editor-in-chief is hoping to double, even triple, our circulation with this story."

"We'll grab a copy on our way back to the hotel," Frank promised.

"Aw, heck. Officer! Excuse me!" Max yelled and waved to a police officer in front of Ollie's shop. "Toss me that newspaper! There, on the ground!"

The officer glanced down at the rumpled paper in the doorway. "Sorry, sir!" he shouted back. "It's evidence!"

"Evidence," Max muttered to us. "It's the biggest story of my career, and that joker calls it evidence. Can you believe it? He's probably just too cheap to buy his own copy! Evidence, my foot."

I shot a glance at Frank and twirled a finger at my temple.

What a fruit loop.

"Mr. Monroe. You said Ollie was poisoned," my brother said, trying to change the subject. "Did you see his body before they put him in the ambulance?"

"You bet I did," answered the reporter, patting his camera. "Got it all on film. He was already dead when they loaded him in. I wanted to get a shot of his face, but he was covered up by the time I got here. I did get a good shot of his cane lying next to him on the stretcher, though."

"How did you hear about it?" Frank asked.

"I didn't. I was on my way here to talk to Ollie. He called and left a message at my office. Said he wanted to talk to me about Mr. X. I show up here just as they're dragging him off to the morgue."

"When did Ollie leave you a message?" Frank asked.

"About a half hour ago," Max told him. Then he narrowed his eyes. "Hey, kid, you should be a reporter. You ask a lot of questions."

Frank smiled nervously. "Well, sir, I'm thinking of studying journalism when I go to college."

"You are?" I asked.

Frank kicked my leg and kept smiling.

"You look like a good kid," said Max. "But here's a little advice. Don't put all your eggs in one basket. Study a whole bunch of subjects. I mean, look at this Ollie guy here. He used to be a big skateboard star. It was his whole life. Then he busted up his leg real bad. Turned into a bitter old man, from what I hear."

"Who do you think killed him?" Frank asked. "And why?"

The reporter rubbed his jaw and shrugged. "My professional opinion? I think Mr. X is just some nutcase looking for attention. When you look at the different victims, the possible motives . . . it just doesn't make sense."

You can say that again, I thought.

"Come on, Joe," said my brother. "Let's grab some lunch."

"Sounds good, man. I'm starved."

Frank reached over and shook hands with the reporter. "It was good to talk to you, Mr. Monroe. Thanks for the advice."

"No problem, kid," said Max, turning back to the crime scene.

Frank and I walked around the corner and found a little Chinese restaurant. We went inside and were quickly seated at a small table under a giant menu on the wall.

After the waitress took our order, I leaned forward and whispered to Frank, "What did I tell you about Max Monroe? The guy is a nutcase. But he's right about Mr. X. Mr. X is a nutcase, too. Because Max *is* Mr. X. There's even an X in his name!"

"Slow down, Joe," Frank said. "I really don't think Max Monroe is crazy. An interesting character, yes. But crazy, no. I think he's telling the truth about getting a message from Ollie and showing up here after the guy was dead. If he had killed Ollie himself, you can be sure he would have taken some pictures of Ollie's face."

Good point, I thought.

"Ollie wanted to talk to a reporter," Frank continued. "He knew something."

"About the Big Air Games?" I asked.

Frank shook his head. "Don't you get it? Ollie knew the identity of Mr. X. And I bet it was something in Max's article that made him figure it out. That's why he called the newspaper."

I had to admit, it made sense.

"We have to get a copy of that paper," I said.

The waitress brought us our order. Frank and I wolfed down our chicken lo mein and moo shu shrimp as fast as we could. We were dying to get a look at the newspaper, but the waitress took forever bringing us our check.

Finally we paid and headed back toward the hotel. We stopped at a newsstand along the way and bought the evening edition of the *Philadelphia Freedom Press.*

I studied the pictures on the front page.

There was a shot of Gongado Lopez being carried on a stretcher; a picture of Jenna, Frank, and me leaning over Jeb Green on the half-pipe; and another one of that paramedic, Carter Bean, giving a thumbs-up through the rear window of the ambulance.

"Dude! We made the front page!" I said.

"Come on," said Frank, pushing me along. "We can read it back at the hotel."

A few minutes later we were crossing the lobby

of the Four Seasons Hotel, weaving our way through the swarming crowd of skateboarders and bikers and other athletes. We walked up to the bald-headed receptionist and asked him if we'd gotten any messages.

He sighed and turned around to check. If possible, he looked even more tired than he had yesterday. "Yes, indeed you do," he said, handing Frank a small pile of envelopes.

Frank thanked the man but didn't examine the envelopes until we were alone in the elevator. "Let's see. What do we have here? Ah. The first one's for you. Very pretty."

He handed me an envelope. My name was handwritten in large swirling letters in hot-pink ink. I opened it and read it out loud.

"Hey, Joe. Thanks for visiting Jeb in the hospital and giving him the flowers. He really appreciated it. He left me a message saying he really liked you guys and was sending you something you might want to see. I don't know what. Anyway, I have an athletes' dinner to go to tonight. Then I plan to crash early. Tomorrow's the big day! See you at the games. Jenna."

"What?" said Frank. "She signed it just 'Jenna'? Not 'Love, Jenna' or 'Yours forever, Jenna'?"

"None of your business," I said, smiling to myself.

We got out of the elevator, went to our hotel room, and flopped ourselves down on one of the beds. I started to read the Mr. X article while Frank opened the second envelope.

"Check this out," said Frank, holding up two plastic-coated badges. "The ATAC team sent us press passes to the games. According to our ID badges, we work for a teen magazine called *Shredder*."

"Cool."

Frank opened the third envelope. It was bigger than the others and stuffed with newspaper clippings.

"What are those?" I asked.

"I'm not sure. Oh wait, here's a note. It's from Jeb." He read it out loud. "'Hi, Frank. Yo, Joe. Thanks for the visit. My mom dropped by right after you left. Get this: She brought all my old scrapbooks for me to look through while I'm getting better. As a kid, I started saving any article I could find about skateboarding. So here I am, flipping through the scrapbooks, and I stumble on some articles about—guess who? Our friend Ollie Peterson. I figured you might want to check them out, so I'm having Mom drop this off at your hotel. Hope you find what you're looking for, dudes. Peace. Jeb.'"

Frank pulled out some of the news clippings and spread them across the bed.

"It was really cool of Jeb to send these," I said. "Too bad we don't need them anymore."

"You never know," said Frank, sifting through the pile. "There might be a valuable clue buried in here."

"He's dead, Frank. You can scratch him off the suspect list."

"Well, Dad once told me that the best way to catch a killer is to investigate the victim. There's usually some sort of link between the two. Murder is hardly ever random."

"Okay, then. Keep looking," I said, turning back to my paper. "And I'll keep reading about Mr. X."

Frank looked up. "See anything interesting?"

I shrugged. "Nothing we didn't already know," I said. "But the photo captions are pretty funny. Listen to this one. Under the picture of us leaning over Jeb, it says, 'Xtreme shock: Freaked-out teens comfort skateboard star and pellet victim Jebediah Green.'"

"'Freaked-out teens'?"

"Yeah. And listen to this. Under that thumbs-up picture of the ambulance guy, it says, 'The Real Hero of the Games: EMT paramedic Carter Bean saves lives and wins hearts of today's troubled youth.'"

"'Troubled youth'? Give me a break," said Frank.

"Maybe you're right about that reporter. He *is* a nut case."

I started to read some more but suddenly remembered something. "Didn't we get a fourth envelope?"

"Oh, yeah," said Frank. "Where did it go?" He looked underneath the news clippings about Ollie. "Here it is. Nice stationery."

He opened it up and read it.

"What is it?"

Frank didn't say anything. He just stared at the note with a stunned look on his face.

"Frank?"

I reached out and took the paper from him. Then I read it.

The message was three simple lines, neatly typed in capital letters.

STOP ASKING QUESTIONS

AND STAY AWAY FROM THE GAMES

IF YOU WANT TO LIVE.

Pretty uncreative for a threatening note. But effective.

10.

Let the Games Begin

As soon as I woke up the next morning, I started getting nervous.

The Big Air Games were about to begin. A crazed killer was on the loose—assaulting, shooting, and poisoning people in the extreme sports world. And we'd received a threat. The mission known as "Extreme Danger" had turned out to be just that.

"Joe! Wake up!" I said, shaking my brother in his bed. "We have a criminal to catch. Come on!"

Joe and I were running out of time—and out of suspects. The newspapers were asking, "Who is Mr. X?" And we didn't have a clue.

"I'm up, I'm up," said Joe, still half asleep. "Where's the bad guy? Let me at him."

"I'm guessing he'll be at the Big Air Games," I said. "And so will we. Get moving."

We showered, dressed, and headed down to the lobby. The hotel had arranged a big continental breakfast for the Big Air guests. All the athletes and fans were there, reading the morning paper and talking about Mr. X.

I glanced down at a copy of the *Freedom Press* on one of the tables. The headline read, MR. X STRIKES AGAIN: EX-SKATEBOARD STAR POISONED!

There were old pictures of Ollie in the prime of his youth—and a new photo of his dead body covered in a sheet right outside his shop.

Joe went to grab us some bagels and juice. I sat down and started to read. A public statement from the police confirmed the presence of poison in the victim's coffee. But Max Monroe's article didn't say anything about Ollie trying to contact the newspaper before he was killed.

"More bad news, huh?" Jenna Cho stood by the table, holding a large glass of juice and a fresh fruit plate. "Mind if I join you?" she asked.

"Have a seat," I said. "Joe is getting us bagels. So I guess you heard about Ollie."

Jenna nodded grimly. "It's so twisted. I mean, the guy was totally obnoxious, but he didn't deserve to be killed."

Joe returned with a big tray in his hands—and a big smile on his face. "Jenna! What's up? Ready for the games?"

"You kidding? I'm ready to win," said Jenna. "The women's freestyle event is this afternoon."

Joe sat down and looked her in the eye. "You know, there's some serious stuff happening right now. I'm a little worried about you."

"Well, I can't quit now," she said. "I've trained too long and too hard. And besides, I like taking risks. The day before yesterday I gave my room number to some strange boy in the lobby."

Joe looked shocked. "What strange boy? Who is he?"

"She's talking about *you*, Einstein," I said without looking up from my newspaper.

We finished our breakfasts and wished Jenna luck before she rushed off to join the other athletes in the shuttle van. Joe and I headed down to the parking garage to get our motorcycles. The Big Air Games were being held in one of the four stadiums in South Philadelphia. The traffic got worse the closer we got, but we made it. We even arrived ahead of schedule.

The stadium complex was a total zoo.

A giant banner greeted us at the entrance: THE CITY OF PHILADELPHIA IS PROUD TO WELCOME THE

BIG AIR GAMES. Hundreds of extreme sports fans were lined up at the gates. Parents with binoculars and kids with skateboards wandered through an obstacle course of food stands and souvenir tables. Some of the sports gear companies were even giving away free hats and T-shirts.

"Outrageous," Joe muttered. "Totally."

I slapped his shoulder and pointed toward a couple of TV news vans. Some men were unloading equipment in front of a large tent. A sign said: PRESS REGISTRATION.

"Come on," I said. "We can use our press passes and skip all these lines."

We steered our motorcycles toward the press tent and parked them next to one of the vans.

"Okay, we're reporters for *Shredder* magazine," I whispered to Joe before we entered the tent.

"Frank! Joe! What are you doing here?"

We should have known Maxwell Monroe would be here too. He waved us over toward the registration desk. We held up our badges to a tall woman who wrote down our ID numbers and said hello to Max.

"You're reporters, too?" he said. "I should have known. You ask too many questions." He chuckled. "So are you ready for big trouble at the Big Air Games?" Max paused for a second. "Hey! I should use that for my next headline! If we're lucky, Mr. X will make a special guest appearance today. Right, boys?"

Jerk.

"Let's go, Joe," I said, grabbing my brother by the arm. "Let's try to get some pregame interviews."

"Catch you later!" Max yelled after us.

The opening ceremonies were about to start. Joe and I quickly found a place near the locker rooms that had a clear view of the field.

A heavyset sportscaster from Channel 7 walked onto the center stage and made some opening remarks. His voice echoed through the loudspeakers. "And without further ado," he said, winding up, "I am honored to introduce you to . . . the extreme sports athletes of the Big Air Games!"

The fans went crazy.

The field exploded with activity. A heavy-metal rock band erupted with sound. Fireworks burst from a cannon. And hundreds of athletes swarmed across the field.

It was hard to know where to look. Inline skaters circled the track. Skateboarders zoomed up and down the long rows of half-pipes. Bungee jumpers were hoisted into the air by gigantic cranes. Then a small army of motocross bikers hurled full-speed into the killer curve of the Monster Loop—up, around, and down—in rapid-fire succession.

"Man! That's insane!" I gasped.

"Look! There's Jenna!" Joe said, pointing toward the half-pipes. She was easy to spot because of her hot-pink skateboard.

"And there's Eddie Mundy," I said. "In the red bandanna."

Joe looked over at the skateboarder. "We should keep an eye on him."

Suddenly all the activity in the field screeched to a halt. The athletes lined up, standing straight and tall, as the band launched into an electric-guitar version of the national anthem.

"Let the games begin!" a voice announced at the end of the song. Some of the athletes started to leave the field.

"Come on, Joe," I said. "Now's our chance. We can talk to the players in the dugouts."

We hurried down the stairs and got as close as we could. A security guard stopped us. "Athletes only beyond this point," he grunted at us. We showed him our press passes. "Maybe they'll let you in the locker rooms."

We walked around to the locker room entrance. Another guard let us through when we flashed our passes.

The men's locker room wasn't very crowded. A few guys were doing stretches. Others were fussing with their gear. One boy with a Mohawk sneered at us. "What are you preppies doing in here?"

"We're reporters," I told him. "Do you mind answering a few questions?"

"Get lost! Go back to your fancy prep school!"

"Yeah!" someone else yelled. "Get in the game or get out!"

Frank tugged my shirtsleeve. "Let's go, Frank," he said. "I have an idea."

When we got outside, Joe hustled me past the guard, then showed me something tucked in his pocket: a pair of official Big Air athletes' passes.

"Where did you get those?"

Joe smiled. "I spotted them under a bench in the locker room. So I snatched them while you were talking to those guys."

I was skeptical. "The security guards saw us, Joe. They think we're reporters, not athletes."

A big smile crept over my brother's face.

"How do you feel about getting an extreme makeover, Frank?"

Before I knew it, we were riding our motorcycles up and down the streets of South Philadelphia, looking for a clothing store. But we weren't having much luck.

Finally Joe pulled over. "Look," he said, pointing across the street. "I bet we can find something in there."

I turned and looked. "You got to be kidding, Joe."

The place was called HOLLYWEIRD.

It looked like a vintage clothing store. There were two mannequins in the window—one in a wedding dress with a hunting vest, the other in a skin-diving suit and a purple wig.

"Come on," Joe said. He wouldn't take no for an answer. We circled around and parked in front of the store.

A little bell tinkled when we walked through the door. Two girls looked up and stared at us. They were sitting in old beauty parlor chairs, reading magazines—and they looked as bizarre as the mannequins in the window.

"Can I help you guys?" asked the tall one. Her hair was bright blue and spiky, and her jeans were held together with safety pins. "I'm Holly."

"And I'm Weird," said the other one. Her face was powdered white, but everything else—hair, lips, clothes—was completely black.

Joe did the talking. "We need to change our look. It could be biker, skateboarder, punk, whatever—as long as it's wild. We want to look . . . you know . . . *extreme.* Can you help us?"

The two girls looked at each other—and grinned from ear to ear.

Grabbing Joe by the shoulders, Holly pushed him toward the changing room and started pulling clothes from a rack. "Here, try these on," she said, handing him a big pile of pants, shirts, and accessories.

The girl named Weird looked at me and motioned with her finger. "Your turn," she said.

"I don't know if I . . ."

It was useless to resist. The girls were thrilled to make us over. We were like a pair of life-sized dolls for them to play with. They made us try on nylon tracksuits, snakeskin pants, flowered surfer shorts— you name it.

Finally, Joe ended up in a black punk-rock concert shirt, oversized army shorts, and a cool racing jacket.

And me? They dressed me in blue camouflage pants, black boots, a tie-dyed tank top, and a leather jacket.

"We approve," said Holly, standing back to admire her work. "You guys look fierce."

I stood next to Joe and looked in the mirror.

Pretty cool, I had to admit.

"You know what would really top it all off?" said Weird, holding up an electric hair trimmer. "Mohawks!"

"Oh, yeah! Totally!" Holly agreed.

I laughed and shook my head. "There's no way I'm going to get a Mohawk."

"I'll do it," said Joe.

I turned to argue, but my brother had already hopped into one of the beauty parlor chairs. Weird spun him around, wrapped a towel around his neck, and plugged in the clippers.

"You, too. Grab a seat," said Holly, pushing me into the other chair.

"Wait! No!" I protested. "I don't want a haircut!"

"Then I'll just spray in some blue dye," she said, picking up an aerosol can. "It washes out . . . and it'll match your pants."

"Go on, Frank," said my brother. "Just do it."

I closed my eyes. "Okay," I said. "Do it."

Holly started spraying—and Weird started shaving.

Bzzzzzzzzzz.

11.

Crash and Burn!

Man! The wind feels cool against my scalp!

I roared along on my motorcycle, right behind Frank, through the streets of Philadelphia. We had gotten a little lost on our trip to Hollyweird, so Frank was using his bike's navigational system to find our way back to the stadium. I followed.

I had to laugh a little at the sight of Frank with blue hair.

Then I reminded myself that I had a Mohawk.

Aunt Trudy and Mom would have my head on a platter.

Well, it was too late to worry about it now. My head was shaved and smooth and shiny, with a spiky stripe of hair down the middle.

Besides, I looked *crazy* cool. And I have to confess: Even *Frank* looked cool.

Finally we spotted the banner for the Big Air Games. Riding past the press tent, Frank and I circled the stadium until we found the athletes' entrance. A security guard held up his arm to stop us. We flashed our passes—the ones I'd swiped from the locker room—and the guard waved us through.

We rode our motorcycles up a large cement ramp and down a long hall. It led us right through the stadium and out onto the south side of the field.

Frank and I must have been quite a sight, because the audience cheered when they saw us.

"Maybe we should pop a few wheelies or something," I said to Frank.

I waved to the crowd. They cheered again.

"Man, I could learn to like this."

"Knock it off, Joe," said Frank, getting off his bike. "Let's go talk to some of the athletes."

"But what about my fans? They want me! Frank! Wait!"

I hopped off my bike and ran after my brother. We walked past a group of inline skaters—and almost collided with Maxwell Monroe.

"Sorry, excuse me," said the reporter. He did a double take. "Hey, wait! It's you guys! Let me check you out! Wow. Great disguises. Now that's one way to infiltrate the inner circle of the extreme sports world. Very clever. I'd try it myself, but I'm too old to pull off a Mohawk or blue hair."

"Lower your volume, Max," I whispered. "You're going to blow our cover."

Max smiled. "Sure, kid. I understand," he said. "We're all journalists here. But let me give you boys a little advice."

Again? He leaned toward us and spoke in a hushed voice. "When Mr. X makes his move today—*and he will*—you don't want to be standing in the line of fire. I'd be careful about getting too close to the athletes if I were you."

Then he said something that sounded strangely familiar.

"And stay off the field . . . if you want to be safe."

I glanced at Frank. He didn't react to Max's words.

"Well, I hope to see you later, boys," the reporter said. "I'm going to the press box. They have sandwiches up there."

We said good-bye and watched Max disappear into the crowd.

"Did you hear that?" I asked Frank. "He used almost the same words as that warning we got: '*And stay away from the games if you want to live.*'"

Frank ran a hand through his blue hair. "Maybe it's just a coincidence," he said.

"Or not," I added. "He seems so sure that Mr. X is going to attack today."

"He's a reporter. Joe. He's *hoping* Mr. X attacks."

We walked around the perimeter of the field as we talked. Soon we came upon the skateboard dugout. I spotted Jenna, so I waved.

She looked at me like I was a total stranger.

Oh, yeah. The Mohawk, I reminded myself.

"Jenna! It's me, Joe!"

She squinted, then smiled and came running out of the dugout. "Look at you guys!" she said. "Extreme Hardys! I like it!" She ran her fingers through my Mohawk.

"Where's your skateboard?" I asked her.

"Over there in the dugout."

"Look," I said. "Keep your skateboard with you at all times. And check the wheels, the axle, everything. Make sure nobody's tampered with the board. And tell the others to do the same. Promise?"

"Promise," she said. Then she told us that her

event would start in about an hour in the stadium next door.

"I'll be there," I told her.

Frank and I said good-bye and started to walk toward the north end of the field. We still hadn't talked to any of the motocross bikers.

Suddenly my brother stopped. "You know what, Joe? What you told Jenna was really smart. No one should leave their equipment unattended."

"Thanks, man," I said. "You never tell me I'm smart. What's the catch?"

"The catch is, we shouldn't leave our motorcycles back there. They could be sabotaged."

"Oh, yeah," I said. "I guess I'm not *that* smart."

Frank laughed. "Come on. Let's get our bikes and ride them up the field."

We turned around and started walking the other way.

"Well, well, well. Check out the posers."

It was Eddie Mundy.

The cocky skateboarder walked right toward us with a big sneer on his face.

Did he ever wash that thing?

Eddie stepped in front of us, blocking our path and giving us the once-over.

"I'm diggin' the new duds. But you still look like

a pair of preppy boys," he teased. "Give it up, dudes. The blue hair and Mohawk aren't fooling anyone."

"Ignore him," Frank whispered. "Just keep moving."

But Eddie wouldn't let it drop.

When we tried to walk around him, he threw his arms over our shoulders and walked along with us.

"Look, guys," he said, lowering his voice. "I know who you are. Really."

I shrugged his hand off. "What are you talking about?" I said. "What did you hear?"

"There you go with the questions again," Eddie said, sighing. "Those questions are getting you both in a lot of trouble. I think you know what I mean."

Frank stopped and stared at him. "What are you saying?" he asked.

Eddie grabbed us both by the arms and squeezed. "I'm saying drop it. Leave. Now."

Then he let go and walked away.

Frank and I didn't say a word for a moment or two. I guess we were a little stunned. Finally I turned to Frank and looked him in the eye.

"Okay," I said. "Things are getting freaky around here. What do you think is going on?"

"I don't know," said Frank. "But I intend to find out."

Clenching his jaw, he stalked off toward our motorcycles at the end of the field. I just stood there and watched him go.

Easy, Frank.

But hey, I wasn't about to let my brother take on Mr. X all by himself. We were a team.

"Frank, wait!" I yelled, running after him.

After stopping to watch one of the bungee jumps, Frank and I reached the south end of the field without incident.

I mean, nobody threatened to kill us if we didn't leave.

Our motorcycles appeared to be okay. But Frank insisted that we inspect them carefully before starting the engines.

"Someone could have cut the brake lines or punctured the gas tanks," he said. "Or a dozen other things."

"Everything checks out," I reported after a quick inspection.

"Check again."

"Frank."

"Check again," he repeated. "This is serious, Joe. People know we've been asking questions. Both

Max and Eddie warned us to back off. Maybe they're concerned. Maybe they're killers. Who knows? We can't take any chances."

Once Frank was satisfied with the inspections, we jumped on our cycles and revved them up. Then we took off, riding slowly along the perimeter of the stadium.

We had to warn the motocross bikers: Don't leave your bikes unattended, not even for a minute.

As we approached the motocross zone, I couldn't stop staring at the huge Monster Loop rising up in the distance.

The thing was humongous!

The highest point of the curve must have been fifty feet high. But as I got closer on my cycle, I swear it seemed more like a hundred. How could anyone get up enough momentum to ride the entire loop without falling?

I was about to find out.

There were six motocross bikers lining up, getting ready to tackle the Monster Loop.

Frank and I pulled up on the sidelines and parked our motorcycles. We jumped off and ran toward the motocross bikers.

"Wait!" Frank yelled. "We need to talk to you!"

We were stopped in our tracks by one of the event directors.

"Hold it right there, boys," he said. "Everyone has to stay back here until the stunts are completed."

Frank tried to explain. He told the event director about the possibility of sabotage and asked if the bikers kept a close watch on their bikes.

"Don't worry, we're taking care of everything," the man assured him. "With Mr. X on the loose, everybody is taking extra precautions. We've got more security, more safety inspectors, more emergency medical teams . . . you name it."

I looked around and saw all the security guards walking along the sidelines—and an ambulance waiting near the Monster Loop. It didn't make me feel any better.

I had seen more than enough medical emergencies in the past two days.

Frank finally gave up trying to get past the event director. He came over and stood next to me, gazing up at the Monster Loop and shaking his head. "That thing is scary."

"Totally."

The motocross bikers were all revved up and ready to roll. Then a man waved a flag and they were off.

The bikers tore up the dirt as they headed for the first series of ramps. Up and over, up and over, the roaring machines sailed through air, then plunged back to earth, wheels spinning faster with every jump.

"Dude!" I shouted out.

The six bikers skidded and swerved past us. Hurtling toward an even bigger ramp, they picked up speed, hit the curve, and shot into the air again, even higher than before.

"All right!" Frank cheered.

Finally the bikers were making their final round—their last chance to build up momentum for the big finish. . . .

The Monster Loop.

Faster and faster, they flew around the track with their engines roaring.

And that's when I noticed something.

One of the bikers' wheels was wobbling.

"Frank!" I yelled. "Look at number four's front wheel!"

We watched helplessly as the biker headed straight for the Monster Loop.

"Stop! No!" my brother and I screamed.

One, two, three of the motocross bikers hit the loop, rising up—thirty, forty, fifty feet in the air—one after the other. Up, up, and over.

Biker number four was right on their heels. The guy must have noticed that his front wheel was wobbling, but it was too late to stop. He hit the curve and rose straight up, his whole bike shaking. Higher and higher he went, until he was nearly upside down at the top of the curve.

"He's not going to make it," Frank gasped. "He's going to fall!"

But no, he didn't fall. The bike completed the upper part of the arch, then plunged its way downward.

That's when the front wheel snapped off.

The front of the bike started grinding into the metal edge of the loop, sparks flying everywhere. The biker tried to lean back—but then the whole bike went tumbling forward, somersaulting down, falling and falling.

Finally biker number four slid to a stop at the bottom of the Monster Loop. The last two bikers managed to swerve out of his way.

But that wasn't the end of it.

Number four's bike burst into flames.

12.

The Biker in Black

I couldn't believe my eyes.

Mr. X had struck again.

And we were too late to stop him.

As the motocross support crew rushed to the burning bike, dousing the flames with fire extinguishers, I lowered my head and replayed the tragedy in my mind.

If only we'd gotten there sooner. We could have warned them. We could have told them to double-check their bikes for sabotage.

I watched in stunned silence as the ambulance pulled up to the scene. Paramedic Carter Bean and his partner, Jack, jumped out and rushed to the biker's side. On the sidelines Monroe held up his camera and clicked away.

I felt like I was reliving the same nightmare, over and over.

Suddenly biker number four sat up, coughed, and threw his hands in the air.

"He's all right! Look!" Joe shouted.

The crowded whooped and cheered.

The biker tried to pick himself up, but Carter and Jack insisted on helping him onto a stretcher. I guess they wanted to make sure he didn't have any broken bones or other injuries. They loaded the guy into the ambulance and turned on the flashing light on the roof. Then they began to drive away.

But not before Maxwell Monroe could snap a few more pictures of Carter and his patient through the rear window.

Everybody—athletes and fans alike—broke into applause as the ambulance left the stadium. I stared down at the ground for a few moments, then looked up at Joe. I didn't know what to say.

"We tried, Frank," he said. "We did everything we could."

"Let's go talk to some of the other bikers," I told him. "Maybe they saw someone suspicious hanging around."

We walked over to a group of guys in motocross jackets standing with the crew. They were all talking about the "accident."

"Do you think it was Mr. X?" one of them said.

"It had to be," said another.

"I can't believe Mike's okay. Did you see how he fell? Head over heels, man!"

"Mike's lucky he's alive."

I interrupted the conversation and asked them if they'd seen anything strange before the race. "Did you notice anyone near the bikes?" I asked. "Someone you didn't know?"

A biker with long hair shook his head. "No, dude," he told us. "There're too many security guys around. Everyone's worried about Mr. X."

Another biker agreed. "The only people I saw had official clearance. You know . . . guards, crew, medics, safety inspectors."

I nodded. The guys went back to talking about Mike McIntyre—biker number four—and his amazing Monster Loop crash. Apparently Mike was not only a star athlete, but also a great guy. Everybody seemed to like him.

"Who's that over there?" I asked, pointing to the sidelines.

In the middle of the crowd was a motocross biker dressed head to toe in black. He sat on a black bike and wore a black helmet, too. The shield was lowered, so I couldn't see his face.

"Huh, I don't know," said the long-haired biker. "Never saw him before."

I turned to ask the other guys if they knew him. They all shook their heads. When I turned back for a second look, the mystery man was gone.

"Frank, we have to go," Joe said, looking at his watch. "It's almost time for Jenna's event."

I wanted to stick around and track down the biker in black—but my brother had promised Jenna we'd be there to cheer her on. Jumping on our motorcycles, we headed for the nearest exit.

We almost didn't make it in time. It took forever to weave our way through the outdoor food stands and vendors to get to the next stadium. But with our athletes' passes, we were able to zip right through and ride our cycles out to the field.

The women's skateboard competition was starting.

"Jenna! Hey!" Joe yelled, spotting her on a bench.

Jenna picked up her skateboard and ran over to meet us. "Hey, guys! You made it!"

"Just barely," I said.

"Man! I am so pumped!" she said with a huge smile. "I'm ready to go for the gold, baby. Look out!" Then her expression changed. "So what's up with you guys? Any sign of Mr. X yet?"

I glanced at Joe.

He shot me a quick look, then smiled at Jenna. "No. Everything's cool," he said. "Go out there and show the world what you can do."

Jenna gave us both a big hug, then dashed back to the bench.

I looked at Joe and raised an eyebrow.

"What?" he said. "I didn't want to give her bad news right now. It could break her concentration."

I smiled. "Joe and Jenna, sittin' in a tree . . ."

"Whatever, Frank."

We watched the first skateboarder, a young girl from Florida. She was incredible, riding the half-pipe like a pro. Then it was Jenna's turn.

I could tell Joe was nervous by the way he clenched and unclenched his hands.

Please, no more accidents, I thought to myself.

Jenna took her place on the edge of the half-pipe. Taking a deep breath, she hopped on her board and went hurtling down the hard concrete curve. She swiveled and swerved, then rode the arch upward, leaping and spinning in the air like a ballerina, smooth and graceful. I'd never seen anyone do skateboard stunts like this before.

"Go, Jenna, go!" Joe shouted beside me.

She ended her routine with a wild 540-degree spin—and the crowd went crazy.

"That's my girl!" Joe hooted.

I turned to tease my brother about his choice of words when I noticed someone on the side-lines.

It was the biker in black.

He sat there on his motocross bike with his arms folded across his chest. He was still wearing his helmet—and shielding his identity. I don't know what it was about him, but he made me itch.

"Joe, look," I said, pointing to the man in black.

Joe spun around.

The mystery man spotted us.

Then he jumped up, kick-started his motocross bike, and took off across the field.

"Come on!" I yelled to Joe. "After him!"

We ran and leaped onto our motorcycles, revving them up as fast as we could. A second later we were racing across the stadium in hot pursuit of the mysterious motocross biker.

The audience cheered and clapped wildly. They must have thought we were part of the games.

But this was no game.

The faster Joe and I went after the guy, the more recklessly he rode—zooming to the left, skidding to the right, then heading straight for the concrete half-pipes.

My brother and I nearly flew off our cycles when we hit the concrete, swerving back and forth between the arching curves like a swinging pair of pendulums.

Finally the biker in black jumped off the final ramp and hit the ground hard, wheels spinning in the turf. Joe and I were right behind him—and he knew it. So he headed for the inline skating track.

My brother and I soared off the last ramp. We both landed hard but managed to steady our bikes and take off after him.

Once we hit the track, the mystery rider didn't stand a chance. His motocross bike didn't have the power or the speed that our motorcycles had.

But he was one step ahead of us. Rounding the bend, he slammed on his brakes and made a hard turn off the track.

Joe and I zoomed right past him—and plunged straight into an inline skating race!

Oops.

Lucky for us, the skaters saw us coming. They veered out of our way, skating to one side or the other so fast that they looked like blurs. Finally we were in the clear.

But where did he go?

Joe and I screeched to a halt and looked around the stadium.

"There he is!" Joe shouted out, pointing across the field.

The biker in black shot out from behind a half-pipe. He headed right for the south exit—and disappeared.

I wasn't about to give up. I nodded at Joe, and we raced to the exit. Rocketing up the ramp, we hurtled headlong into a dark hallway. People screamed and jumped out of our way. Seconds later we were out of the stadium—and lost in a maze of food stands and vendors.

Where was he?

I skidded to a stop, my rear wheel swerving beneath me and bashing into a ring toss booth. Dozens of stuffed animals showered down on me.

"Sorry, ma'am," I said to the startled booth lady. "I'll pay for this. I promise."

I hopped back on my bike and rode slowly through the crowd until I found my brother.

Eating a hot dog.

"Joe!"

"Hey, I was hungry!" he said, taking a bite.

I was about to respond when I spotted the biker in black. "There he is! He's going into the main stadium!"

Joe shoved the rest of the hot dog into his saddlebag. "For later," he explained.

We revved up again and headed for the athletes' entrance. Minutes later we were inside the stadium, searching for the mystery rider.

"Frank! I see him!"

My brother pointed me toward the motocross track. Our mystery man was trying to blend in with the other bikers. But since he was the only guy wearing all black, his plan didn't work.

Joe and I raced up the field after him. As soon as he saw us coming, he revved up his engine and hit the racetrack at full speed.

We kicked into high gear and followed him. In seconds we were gaining on him—until we hit the first series of ramps. The speed of our motorcycles sent us flying too high and too far into the air. We landed with a bone-crunching thud on the top of each ramp, our bikes bucking with each jolt.

Ow.

Back on level ground, we were able to pick up speed again, closing in fast on our target. But the mystery rider was going straight for the last and largest ramp—and he was totally gunning it.

Up, up, and into the air he soared, with Joe and me right behind him.

Whoa! Watch out!

For a second I thought we were going to land right on top of him. Flying and falling, I looked below me. The biker bounced out of the way in the nick of time—and kept right on going. But Joe and I were hot on his heels.

From this point on, it was full speed ahead.

Straight into the Monster Loop.

No, I thought. *Not that.*

There was no turning back. We were just too close—and going too fast.

The three of us hurtled into the giant upward curve of the Monster Loop—the biker first, then Joe, then me. The roar of our engines echoed inside the loop. I watched Joe and the biker go up, up, up, higher and higher, until they were no longer in front of me—they were *above* me.

My stomach turned.

And so did we.

The whole world, it seemed, was rolling beneath my wheels. I glanced down and saw nothing but blue sky below me. At first I didn't understand. Then it hit me.

I was upside down!

But not for long. Soon we were plunging downward on the other side of the loop. Joe and the motocross biker were right below me.

We were coming down to earth now—and *fast.*

The mystery rider plunged downward and outward. Swerving and wobbling, he hit the level ground, rode straight out of the loop—and totally wiped out.

Joe and I had to hit our brakes as hard as we could to avoid hitting the guy.

Finally we came to a stop. Jumping off our cycles, we dashed over to the fallen biker in black.

He lay on the ground next to his bike and moaned. But he didn't seem to be injured, because when he saw us, he jumped to his feet and tried to run away.

Joe and I grabbed him and held on tight.

"Okay, mystery rider," I said. "Let's see who you are."

Joe reached up and pulled off the biker's helmet.

I couldn't believe it.

13.

"Meet Me at Midnight"

Frank and I had risked our lives, raced with death—*even rode the Monster Loop*—and for what?

To unmask a mystery man who turned out to be . . .

Chet Morton?

Chet was one of our best friends from home and, until now, we'd never seen any hint of his wild side. He was definitely the last person I expected to see underneath that black helmet.

"You're not Mr. X," said Frank.

"More like Mr. Y," I said. "As in *W-H-Y* are you here, Chet?"

Chet looked embarrassed. "I dropped by your house yesterday, and your mom said you were at the Big Air Games. At first I was a little insulted.

Why didn't you ask me to come along? Then I figured you must be working on a case. So I decided to help you out and go undercover. Just like you."

He pointed at my Mohawk and Frank's blue hair.

"When you spotted me, I guess I freaked out," he went on. "I was afraid you'd think I was a suspect."

"Well, yeah," I said. "We did."

Just then the biker crew and medical team swarmed around Chet to see if he was okay. Joe and I backed away from the crowd.

"What are we going to do with him?" I asked Frank. "Chet could ruin the whole mission."

Frank shrugged. "Maybe he could help us out," he said. "It wouldn't be the first time."

"Yeah, but he helped us out when we were amateur detectives. We're on the ATAC team now, Frank. These are serious missions . . . with major risks involved."

Frank looked at me. "Did you see how he jumped those giant ramps and tore into that Monster Loop? You have to admit, Joe. The guy is fearless."

Maybe Frank had a point.

A few minutes later—after Chet convinced the paramedics that he didn't need to go to the emergency room—we invited our friend to stay with us in our hotel room, if he needed a place to crash.

"Can I? Cool!" he answered.

We decided to hang out for a while and watch a few more events—but then I remembered something.

Jenna.

I told Frank and Chet that I wanted to go back to the other stadium. They weren't thrilled about riding through that maze of food stands and vendors again, but once I told them why I wanted to go, they agreed. Believe it or not, Chet's bike was still in working order.

As we slowly rode our way out of the stadium, Maxwell Monroe started shouting to us from the press box.

"Joe! Frank! I want to talk to you guys!" he yelled at the top of his lungs.

Frank rolled his eyes. "He probably wants to interview us about our little bike chase," he said.

Neither of us was in the mood to answer the reporter's questions. So I waved back at Max, pointed to my watch, and shook my head. Then we rode our bikes through the exit and headed for the other stadium.

Jenna was thrilled to see us.

"I was so worried about you guys," she said. "What was up with that crazy bike chase? Who were you chasing?"

We introduced her to Chet.

"So? Did you win?" I asked her.

Jenna held up a medal. "Second place!"

I gave her a big hug. "Congratulations," I said. "Second place, huh? That's great."

"Yeah. But it's not first place."

"Hey, there's always next year."

"Will you come to watch me?" she asked.

"Of course," I replied.

"Promise?"

"Promise."

I also promised to join Jenna and some of her skateboard buddies later that night to celebrate her victory. Frank and Chet were invited too, of course.

The four of us found some seats and watched a few more events. My favorite was the skysurfing contest. The competitors were actually dropped from planes overhead. These dudes "surfed" through the air, doing all kinds of crazy spins and twirls, before landing with their parachutes right in the middle of the stadium. It was totally awesome.

I would have enjoyed it even more if my own parachute cord hadn't been cut the other day.

The rest of the games were pretty uneventful, which was cool with me. By the time we got back to the hotel, Frank, Chet, and I were pretty hungry and tired. We flopped down on the beds and considered ordering in some food.

That's when Frank noticed the blinking light on the hotel phone.

"We got a message," he said, picking it up and pushing a few keys on the touchtone pad.

Frank listened for a minute. Then his face turned white.

"Frank? What is it?" I asked.

Slowly he handed me the receiver and pushed a couple of keys to replay the message. I put the phone to my ear and listened.

"Hello, Frank, Joe."

The voice was scratchy and muffled. It creeped me out.

"I know the identity of Mr. X."

I sucked in my breath and waited to hear more.

"Mr. X, you see, is misunderstood. You should be thanking him, really. Would you like to know more about him?"

There was a long pause. The voice got deeper.

"Meet me at midnight. Tonight. In Love Park. And don't call the police. This will be our little secret."

Click.

That was it. End of message.

I handed the phone back to Frank.

"Who was that?" asked Chet.

"Nobody," I told him.

"Well," said Chet, "it seems like *nobody* just scared the living daylights out of you two. What's up?"

"Should I tell him, Frank?" I asked my brother.

Frank sat down on his bed, staring at the scattered press clippings about Ollie's tragic career. He seemed to be lost in thought. "Okay," he finally said. "Let's tell him."

We ordered up three Philly cheese steaks from the hotel's room service and spent the next hour filling Chet in on all the details of the Mr. X case. Of course, we didn't tell him we were on an undercover mission for American Teens Against Crime. ATAC was a top-secret organization, and he wouldn't have heard about it, anyway.

"Let me get this straight," said Chet. "Mr. X has attacked four people, one of whom is dead. He sent you a warning to stop asking questions if you want to stay alive. And now you plan on meeting this wacko in a park tonight at midnight?"

Frank sighed and nodded. "Yup. That pretty much sums it up."

"Cool," said Chet. "Can I come with you?"

"No," I said. "It's too risky."

Frank looked at me. "We *could* use a lookout, Joe," he said. "He could stand back and watch from a distance. That way, if there's any trouble . . ."

"I jump in and start kicking butt!" said Chet, striking his goofiest kung fu pose.

"No, you call the police," said Frank. "Deal?"

"Deal."

"Okay. Everybody synchronize your watches."

Exactly four hours and thirty-seven minutes later, we were standing in a dance club near John F. Kennedy Plaza and celebrating Jenna's second-place victory. Her skateboard friends were really cool and lots of fun. They loved going wild on the dance floor. The music was kicking, the lights were flashing—and Chet, to everyone's surprise, turned out to be a moving, grooving, one-man dancing machine.

"Come on, Frank!" he shouted to my brother sitting near the bar. "Get up and boogie!"

I could tell Frank was nervous.

So was I. But I tried to hide it so I could show Jenna a good time.

"Jenna, do you know a place called Love Park?" I shouted over the music while we danced. "Is it close to JFK Plaza?"

"It *is* JFK Plaza," she answered. "Everyone calls it Love Park. The place is part of skateboard history, one of the coolest spots on the planet for doing street stunts. It's legendary. But nowadays the police arrest people for skateboarding there. Still, that doesn't stop some kids. They'll risk anything so they can tell everyone they skated at Love Park. It's like a badge of honor."

I narrowed my eyes. "Have *you* ever skated at Love Park?" I asked her.

Jenna smiled mysteriously. "A woman never reveals her deepest secrets," she said.

Frank came up behind me and tapped my shoulder. He pointed at his watch.

Almost time.

I told Jenna that we had to leave now. It was getting late.

"Don't go," she pleaded. "It's not even midnight yet."

I apologized and promised to talk to her tomorrow. Then Frank, Chet, and I headed out of the club and into the darkened streets of Philadelphia.

"I thought we should get there early to find a hiding place for Chet," Frank explained as we walked down the sidewalk toward the park.

It was a hot, muggy night. The air was damp, and the atmosphere was thick. Heavy gray storm clouds settled over the city, raising the temperature. Even the streetlamps, with their dull hazy glow, seemed to feel the heat.

"There it is, over there," said Frank. "Love Park."

I started to sweat. We were about to meet Mr. X—or at least someone who claimed to *know* Mr. X. I thought about that strange raspy voice on the phone message, and I shuddered.

We walked toward the huge round fountain in the center of the plaza. I watched a tall geyser of water shoot up into the air. Then I turned and scanned the rest of the park. It was easy to see why the place would be a skateboarder's dream. There were marble benches and steps and ledges everywhere—perfect for street skating.

Frank stopped in front of a tall modern sculpture. "I guess this is why it's called Love Park," he said.

I looked up at the cube-shaped structure. It was made of four giant letters cast in steel—a large L and a tilted O stacked on top of a V and an E. It looked like a design from the 1960s.

"Maybe you can hide right here, Chet, in the shadow of the sculpture," said Frank. "Joe and I will circle the fountain until Mr. X shows up."

Chet nodded and crouched down at the base.

"How's this?" he asked. "Can you see me?"

"Not if you stay in the shadows," Frank told him. "Just stay low and keep an eye out for us. Do you have your cell phone with you?"

"Cell phone. Check," said Chet.

"Okay. It's almost midnight. Let's go, Joe."

We headed quickly and quietly toward the fountain. The city lights bounced off the rippling water and cast tiny flickers of orange and blue across the park. We stopped at the low curving edge of the stone landmark.

I gazed across the street to see if there was anyone on the sidewalk.

Where are you, Mr. X? We're ready for you. Come out and play.

I couldn't see a soul. And I couldn't hear a thing either—just the gurgling jet sprays of the fountain.

"I don't like the looks of this," I whispered. "I think we're being set up."

"Just hang in there, Joe," said my brother. "It's almost midnight."

Slowly and steadily we circled the fountain until we reached the far side of the plaza. A low rumble of thunder rolled overhead.

Suddenly Frank stopped.

"Turn around," he said. "Let's go back."

"Why?" I asked.

"The fountain is blocking the view. Chet can't see us here."

We couldn't see Chet either.

But we could hear him.

"Frank! Joe!"

It sounded like he was struggling. A loud scream echoed across the plaza.

14.
A Real Shocker

It's Mr. X. He's here.

Joe and I dashed to the other side of the fountain as fast as we could. A sudden flash of lightning lit up the park.

"Chet!" Joe shouted. "Hold on! We're coming!"

I heard footsteps running off as we circled the plaza and sprinted toward the Love statue.

Where's Chet?

I could only make out a dark shape lying in the shadows. A bolt of lightning flashed again—and revealed the still body of our friend underneath the sculpture.

"Chet!"

Joe reached him first. Dropping to his knees, he pressed his ear against Chet's chest. "He's still alive," he shouted, his voice echoing through the park. "Call 911!"

I pulled out my cell phone. "Hello, we have an emergency here!" I barked. "A boy's been hurt in JFK Plaza! Under the Love statue! Send an ambulance!"

I crouched down next to Joe and leaned over to examine Chet. "I don't see any serious injuries," I said. "He's breathing okay."

Joe stood up and scanned the park. Another boom of thunder rumbled overhead, but louder than before.

"The storm's about to break," Joe said. "And Mr. X is still out there. He's probably watching us right now."

I felt a drop of rain on my hand.

A siren wailed in the distance. It sounded like it was only a block or two away—and getting closer. Thirty seconds later, I spotted the ambulance. It barreled down the street, lights flashing, and pulled up to the curb. The door flew open. Carter Bean hopped out from the driver's seat and raced toward us.

Chet let out a little groan. Slowly turning his head and blinking his eyes, he gazed up at Carter. His eyes widened.

I jumped up and stood in between Chet and the paramedic.

"Hello, Carter," I said. "Or should I call you Mr. X?"

Thunder and lightning filled the sky. The storm was ready to hit—and it was going to be a big one.

SUSPECT PROFILE

Name: Carter Bean

Hometown: Philadelphia, PA.

Physical description: 35 years old, 6'3", 165 pounds, thin wiry build, short brown hair, hazel eyes

Occupation: EMT paramedic, Pennsylvania Hospital

Background: Grew up in poor neighborhood in Philadelphia, worked his way through medical school, became local hero for saving skateboard legend Ollie Peterson's leg after 1990 accident

Suspicious behavior: Treated every victim in the Big Air Games attacks (unlikely in a city this size)

Suspected of: Assault, battery, sabotage, and murder

Possible motives: To draw attention away from extreme sports heroes, relive past glory, gain fame and recognition for lifesaving work

The rain came down hard and heavy, but in spite of the sudden downpour, nobody moved.

Carter Bean glared at me, his eyes narrowing. "What are you talking about?" he said. "I'm here to help. You called 911, didn't you?"

I looked Carter straight in the eye. "No, I didn't," I said. "I just pretended to call. I knew you would show up anyway."

The paramedic smirked. "How did you know? What proof do you have?"

"I saw your picture in the old news clippings of Ollie's accident in 1990," I explained. "You got a lot of press coverage, didn't you? How did the newspaper put it? Oh, yeah. 'A Legend Falls. A Hero Is Born.'"

"So?" said Carter, blinking the rain out of his eyes. "Everyone in the medical profession is a hero. I was just getting the recognition I deserved."

"Maybe," I said. "But real heroes don't do it for the recognition. Real heroes do the right thing because it's the right thing to do. They don't plan 'accidents' . . . like you did at the Big Air Games."

"Like I said before. What proof do you have?"

"Oh, come on. Every time someone got hurt, you were right there, ready to jump out of your ambulance and save the day."

Carter scoffed and shoved his hands in his pockets. "That doesn't prove that I attacked anybody. It's just a coincidence."

I pointed to his medical ID badge. "Is that a coincidence, too? Your ID number is EMT7654. But backward, it's 4567TME. That's the name you used to post threats on the Internet."

Carter sneered. "You think you're pretty smart, don't you?" he said. "I must admit—I'm stunned by your cleverness. Absolutely stunned. And I think I should return the favor."

He pulled a small stun gun from his pocket and thrust it straight at my throat.

"Frank! Look out!" Joe yelled.

I ducked fast. The stun gun swooped over my head with an electric crackle and a little zap of light.

Carter cursed me and lunged again. I tried to sidestep his attack but my knee slammed against the base of the Love sculpture. The impact sent me spinning and stumbling to the ground.

Carter stood over me. "Be a good patient now and take your medicine," he said.

He lowered the stun gun to my shoulder.

Joe tackled him to the ground.

Get him, Joe!

The two of them hit the wet concrete and rolled

across a puddle. Carter held the stun gun between them, aiming it at Joe's face.

I crawled to my feet and limped toward them. My knee throbbed with pain.

The stun gun buzzed in Carter's hand, a tiny bolt of electricity sizzling at the tip. Joe gripped the guy's wrist, struggling to push it away.

"Don't be afraid, kid," Carter growled. "It's just a little electroshock therapy."

The stun gun moved closer to Joe's face.

I staggered forward—but I knew I wouldn't make it in time to save Joe.

"Hey, Carter! Think fast!" I yelled.

I threw my cell phone like a baseball. It hit the paramedic in the ear, knocking his head back.

And he's out!

But no, Carter Bean was still in the game. Even though he lost his grip on Joe, he held on tight to the stun gun. In seconds the paramedic was up on his feet and waving the defense weapon like a sword.

Joe jumped back with every swoop of Carter's arm. The rain pounded, even harder than before. My brother almost slipped and fell as Carter forced him backward toward the fountain.

"Careful, kid," he said. "Accidents happen every day."

I had to do something—and fast. My knee throbbed, but I had to help my brother.

The lightning illuminated the way as I staggered after them. "Carter! I called the cops! They're on the way!"

"Liar!" Carter shouted, taking another lunge at Joe. "You threw your phone at me! Remember?"

He zapped the stun gun near my brother's head, forcing Joe back to the edge of the fountain. I limped forward as fast as I could, until I was right behind them.

I threw my arm around Carter's neck.

He spun around and kicked me in the knee.

I went down.

But Joe managed to get away. Slipping to the side, he took a few steps back, then charged full-force at our opponent.

Carter was too fast for him. He swung his right hand—stun gun blazing—at my brother's neck. When Joe tried to block it, Carter brought up his left fist and punched my brother in the jaw.

Joe reeled back—and collapsed to the ground.

"Joe!" I shouted.

He didn't move. It looked like he was unconscious.

Carter turned to me and smiled. "Looks like this is it, Frank. If you think you can get away from me now, you're in for a real shocker." He came after me with the stun gun.

I didn't stand a chance. My knee was hurting even more now. When I tried to scramble away, Carter stepped down on my leg and pinned me to the ground.

I stared up helplessly, the rain stinging my eyes.

Carter pointed the stun gun at my head.

"It's a shame, really," he said. "No matter how hard a paramedic tries to save lives, some patients just don't pull through."

He brought the stun gun closer to my face. Blazing sparks of electricity danced on the tip. He aimed it at my neck and . . .

Wham!

Carter was knocked off his feet.

A bright streak of red zoomed past me. A set of wheels skidded on the wet concrete.

It was Eddie Mundy!

The skateboarder in the red bandanna had plowed right into the paramedic. Carter was flat on his back, groaning.

"Eddie? What are you doing here?" I asked.

"I'm not who you think I am," he said, skating around the fallen paramedic. As Eddie started to explain, I saw Carter's arm move.

He still had the stun gun!

"Eddie! Look out!" I shouted.

Carter jabbed the weapon at Eddie's leg. The skateboarder kicked down hard on the back of his board. The front end flew up, slamming into Carter's arm and knocking him down.

The stun gun went flying into the fountain.

"Nice job," I said.

Eddie helped me to my feet. I had to lean against him for support because of my knee—not to mention the fact that my clothes were totally drenched and felt like they weighed a ton. I looked over at my brother. Joe was sitting up in a puddle, rubbing his jaw and smiling.

"Did we get him?" he asked.

"Yeah," I said. "Eddie skated right over the guy like he was a half-pipe."

"Eddie?"

The skateboarder offered Joe a hand and helped him up. "Actually, I'm an ATAC agent, just like you guys," Eddie said.

"Dude!" Joe exclaimed. "We thought you were bad news, man. You threatened us at the games today."

"I was warning you," Eddie explained. "Back at ATAC headquarters, they were afraid you two were going to be Mr. X's next targets."

"Turns out they were right," said Joe. "Hey, where is that psycho nurse anyway?"

Eddie and I spun around.

Carter was gone.

"Later, boys!" a voice rung out from the other side of the fountain. "I have to go now. It's an emergency!"

Carter laughed as he dashed around the fountain, heading for his ambulance. Eddie started running after him, with Joe and me staggering behind.

There's no way we can catch him.

Then I heard something strange. The rumbling sound of wheels seemed to be circling the plaza. Suddenly, out of the darkness came a whole gang of skateboarders, bounding down steps, grinding across benches, and jumping off curbs. They headed straight for Carter Bean and surrounded him, a human fence of skateboarders, zooming so fast that their prisoner couldn't escape.

"Look! There's Jenna!" Joe pointed out. "And her friends! They must have followed us out of the club."

Just then a small brigade of police cars came speeding down the street. One of them blared its siren, and they all pulled up to the curb and stopped. There must have been a dozen officers. Most of them charged at the skateboarders, breaking up the circle and apprehending the suspect. Two of them ran to the Love statue to help Chet, and the others came over to Eddie, Joe, and me. "Are you boys all right?" a tall officer asked. "Sorry it took us so long to track down that missing ambulance."

"Missing ambulance?" I asked.

"We wanted to question Carter Bean," the officer explained. "When the hospital tried to find him, they discovered he was gone—and one of their ambulances was missing."

Chet came over to join us. He looked a little stunned—no pun intended. "How did the police get here so fast?" he asked.

"You didn't call them?" asked Joe.

"No, I never got the chance. I got jumped by some guy with a stun gun. He must have stolen my cell phone."

"So who called the police?" I asked.

"I did," said a voice behind us.

It was Maxwell Monroe.

The reporter strolled up and smiled. "I had reasons to suspect Bean," he told us. "After Ollie was killed, I dug up all the old articles about him in our records. Then I saw that Carter Bean was the ambulance hero who saved Ollie's leg, and I got suspicious. But I didn't have enough to go on for a cover story. So I told the cops they should question the guy. You can read all about it in tomorrow's paper."

My mind was reeling with questions. But I never had a chance to ask them. Carter Bean started yelling as two of the police officers tried to handcuff him.

"Careful! You're hurting me!" he cried. "You're hurting me!"

"Well, Carter," I said. "Maybe you should call 911."

15.

Heroes

Okay. So we caught the bad guy. Mr. X was safely behind bars. The Big Air Games were a huge success. Our mission was accomplished.

Still, I was totally confused. Why was Ollie poisoned? Why didn't Carter save Ollie's life, like he did for the others?

"Maybe Eddie Mundy can tell us," Frank said.

We got up early the next morning and sneaked out of the hotel room while Chet was still sleeping. We had agreed to meet Eddie at an out-of-the-way diner to discuss the details of the case. He was already waiting for us when we arrived.

"Eddie! My man!" I said. "Looking good, dude."

Without the red bandanna, Eddie was like a

totally different person. His hair was neatly combed, and instead of skateboard gear, he wore a button-down shirt and khaki pants.

Frank and I, of course, still had the blue hair and the Mohawk.

"Hey, Frank, Joe," he said as we slid into the booth. "I think I owe you guys an apology. I thought you knew I was an ATAC agent after I dropped that hint."

"What hint?" I asked.

"In FDR Park, I said it was 'extremely dangerous' to ask questions," he explained. "From the looks on your faces, I thought you understood. I was referring to the name of our mission."

"Actually," I said, "that only made me suspicious. You?" I looked at Frank. "Definitely," he agreed. "But now I get it."

Then we asked Eddie about the murder of Ollie Peterson. We wondered why it seemed different from the other attacks. Why would Carter want Ollie dead?

"Here's our theory," Eddie began. "Ollie may have resented Carter for becoming a hero after the accident in 1990. Some of the papers barely mentioned Ollie's awards and reputation in the skateboarding community. They focused on this young resourceful paramedic, fresh out of school. He was a poor kid from Philly who worked a bunch of night jobs to pay for medical school . . . an everyday hero who saved a man's leg and looked good in photographs."

Frank and I nodded.

"Okay, so years later, Ollie has his own skateboard shop," Eddie continued. "He probably forgot all about the kid who got famous from his tragedy. Then one day Ollie buys the evening edition of the *Freedom Press,* and there's that same paramedic—and he's a big hero again. So what does Ollie do? Well, we traced his phone records and found out that he called information and got Carter's number. He called Carter and talked for two minutes, then dialed up the *Freedom Press.*"

"Maxwell Monroe told us that Ollie left a message at his office," said Frank. "He wanted to talk to the reporter about Mr. X."

"Ollie obviously suspected Carter Bean," said Eddie. "We believe that he called Carter on the phone to question him or accuse him—or maybe just harass him. Either way, Carter felt threatened. Ollie had to be silenced. So Carter stole some medication from the hospital and slipped a fatal dose into Ollie's coffee."

I let it all sink in. "Okay," I said. "That explains Ollie. How did you know we were meeting Mr. X at midnight in Love Park?"

"I was following you," Eddie answered. "I was even there in the dance club last night. Man, your friend Chet is one crazy dancer."

"He's also the mystery biker in black," I added.

"That was some mean riding," said Eddie, laughing. "I freaked when I saw you guys head for the Monster Loop."

"*You* freaked?" said Frank.

I asked Eddie another question. "What about Jenna and her friends? They all scattered when the cops showed up. But why were they there in the first place?"

Eddie gave me a sly smile. "You'll have to ask Jenna yourself."

"I plan to."

We talked a little more about ATAC and some of our missions. When it was finally time to go, Eddie reached under the table and pulled out a box.

"I have a little souvenir for you guys."

He slid it across the table. I laughed when I saw the wrapping paper. It was the front page of the *Philadelphia Freedom Press*. The headline read, MR. X

X-POSED! MANIAC MEDIC BUSTED BY DAREDEVIL DUO. There was a picture of Carter in handcuffs next to one of Frank and me chasing Chet through the Monster Loop.

"Open it," said Eddie.

We tore away the paper and laughed again. It was a first aid kit full of bandages.

"I found it on the curb last night next to Carter's ambulance," Eddie explained.

We thanked Eddie for the memento and rushed back to the hotel. Then we dashed up to our room to pack our stuff and check out.

We'd almost forgotten about Chet. He was still sleeping—and snoring and mumbling. I had to laugh. And I had to mess with him a little too. So I took a long gauze bandage from the first aid kit and tied a big bow in his hair.

"Shouldn't we wake him?" Frank asked. "We can't just leave him here like this."

"But he looks so peaceful," I said.

"And so pretty," Frank added.

We sneaked out of the room, trying not to laugh too hard. Then we headed to the elevator with our backpacks and helmets. Jenna had left a message that she'd meet us in the lobby at ten o'clock—and she had a surprise for us. When we got downstairs, we found her sitting on the steps with Jebediah Green.

"Jeb! Dude!" I said. "How are you feeling?"

"Not bad. Just a little sore," Jeb said with a smile. "How's the Daredevil Duo?"

Frank rubbed his knee and winced. "Just a little sore. Thanks for sending us those clippings, man. They helped us figure out who Mr. X was."

"Ah, yes. The Maniac Medic," said Jeb, holding up a copy of the *Freedom Press*. "That's one twisted dude."

While Frank and Jeb laughed over the headlines, I took Jenna aside to say good-bye. We swapped e-mail addresses and home phone numbers and agreed to stay in touch. I promised to visit her in Atlantic City before the end of the summer. Then Frank interrupted, saying we had to hit the road now.

I looked into Jenna's eyes, hating to say good-bye. "Tell me something," I said. "Why did you follow me to Love Park last night with your skateboard buddies?"

"Because I knew you were looking for trouble," she answered. "And because I wanted to help out. And because I care about you."

I smiled. "Good answer."

She cares about me!

Frank cleared his throat. "Time to go," he said.

Jenna kissed me on the cheek and gave Frank a hug. Then we waved good-bye to Jeb and headed down to the parking garage. On the way I noticed that Frank was quieter than usual. I asked him what was up.

"I don't know," he said, shrugging. "Maybe I'm just a little jealous. I mean, the mission's over, and you have this new friend who just happens to be a gorgeous girl and an extreme skateboard champ. And what do I have?"

I tried to cheer him up. "You have a parrot waiting at home for you, Frank."

He reached over and messed up my Mohawk.

The ride home was a nice way to unwind after the extreme dangers of our mission. The sky was clear and blue, and our motorcycles—I swear—seemed to enjoy cutting loose on the wide-open highway. In just a couple of hours we roared into our hometown and turned down the road to our house.

Aunt Trudy's Volkswagen was sitting in the driveway looking good as new. Dad must have driven it through a car wash after he had it fixed. I was glad the repairs hadn't taken long. As a joke, my brother and I parked our motorcycles right behind the VW, blocking it in. Just to drive Aunt Trudy a little crazy.

"Home sweet home," said Frank, pulling off his helmet and fluffing his hair.

"It's our *crib*, Frank. Get with the times." I took off my helmet and followed him to the porch.

The old house looked exactly the same.

Frank and I, however, did not.

Mom screamed when she saw us. "Oh, my gosh! What did you boys do to your hair? Frank! You're blue!"

Frank walked across the living room and gave her a kiss. "You dye your hair too, Mom."

"I do not."

"I've seen you touch up the gray."

"Not me. I don't have any gray hair. And if I did, I wouldn't dye it blue. Green, maybe, but never blue. And *you!*" she said, pointing at my head. "What made you think it's the 1980s? You're not in a punk band. People don't wear Mohawks anymore."

"Sure they do, Mom," I said, giving her a kiss. "Your son wears one."

Dad sat in his chair, laughing. He was always happy when we got home safe and sound after a mission—and always a little concerned. "Welcome back," he said. "I can't wait until your Aunt Trudy sees you boys."

"Where is she?" I asked.

My dad rolled his eyes. "Actually, you might want to hop back on your bikes and travel across the country for a while."

"Why? What's up with Aunt Trudy?" asked Frank.

Mom started to laugh. "Ask your parrot."

Just then, we heard a bloodcurdling shriek upstairs—and the flapping of wings.

"Get off of me!" Aunt Trudy screamed. "Get your stinking claws off me, you darn dirty bird! Off! Off!"

Playback came swooping down from the staircase and flew around the room. The parrot circled three times, squawked, then landed on top of Frank's new blue hairdo.

"Playback! Don't mess with the hair! I just styled it!" Frank lifted the parrot off his head and set him down on the mantel above the fireplace.

I heard footsteps coming down the stairs. Frank and I turned around to greet Aunt Trudy.

"I've had just about enough," she was saying. "Those boys better bring back a cage for that winged demon or I'm going to . . . AAAAAUUUGH!!! Stay back, you, or I'll chop you in half, I swear! I know judo!"

Aunt Trudy waved her arms wildly in the air.

"Aunt Trudy, it's us," said Frank, laughing.

Our aunt stopped waving and squinted at us. "Of course I knew it was you. I was just . . . just playing along." She straightened her shirt and hugged us. "Did you remember to get me the Band-Aids?"

I reached into my backpack and handed her the first aid kit that Eddie had given us.

"Oh, my, these look so professional. Like the kind you see in hospitals. Thank you very much."

"Oh, it was nothing," I said.

Frank glanced at me and laughed. We turned to go upstairs and unpack.

"Wait, I'm not done with you two yet," said Aunt Trudy. She disappeared into the kitchen and returned with a bucket of warm soapy water.

"What's this?" I asked.

"This is for cleaning up after that parrot of yours," she explained, handing us each a sponge. "I told you that bird was going to poop all over the house. Look! Right here on the table! And look! On the carpet! And oh my goodness, look! He's pooping right now on the mantel!"

Frank and I started laughing.

"Well, if you think it's so funny, then you should have a load of laughs cleaning it up," said Aunt Trudy. "And you might think about using the sponge on your hair while you're at it!"

Frank and I took the bucket and sponges and started scrubbing the mantel. What could we do?

Dad turned on the television. "Boys! Look! It's the Big Air Games!" Frank and I turned to see the videotaped footage of our Monster Loop jump, ending with the helmeted Chet's wipeout.

Mom shook her head. "Anyone who would do something like that is just crazy," she said.

"But Mom, that's the Daredevil Duo and their sidekick, Hatchet," I said, winking at Frank.

"I don't care *who* they are. If you want to talk about *real* courage, I saw something on the news yesterday about this paramedic who saved two of those extreme sports kids at the park. Now that's what the world needs today. Real heroes."

Playback squawked.

"Heroes! Heroes! Heroes!"

Frank and I looked at each other.

"Get back to work, boys!" said Aunt Trudy. "That poop isn't going to clean itself up."

Cleaning up crime? I'm into it. Cleaning up parrot poop? Not so much. But hey, a job's a job. Glancing at Frank's hair, I smiled and went back to sponging.

Exciting fiction from three-time Newbery Honor author Gary Paulsen

PENDRAGON

Bobby Pendragon is a seemingly normal fourteen-year-old boy. He has a family, a home, and a possible new girlfriend. But something happens to Bobby that changes his life forever.

HE IS CHOSEN TO DETERMINE THE COURSE OF HUMAN EXISTENCE.

Pulled away from the comfort of his family and suburban home, Bobby is launched into the middle of an immense, interdimensional conflict involving racial tensions, threatened ecosystems, and more. It's a journey of danger and discovery for Bobby, and his success or failure will do nothing less than determine the fate of the world. . . .

PENDRAGON

by D. J. MacHale

Book One: The Merchant of Death
Book Two: The Lost City of Faar
Book Three: The Never War
Book Four: The Reality Bug
Book Five: Black Water

Coming Soon: Book Six: The Rivers of Zadaa

From Aladdin Paperbacks • Published by Simon & Schuster